D0807434

BISON
BOOKS

NIGHT AND DAY . . . GROUPS WERE TO BE SEEN

THE CHASE

OF THE

GOLDEN METEOR

BY

JULES VERNE

ILLUSTRATED

Introduction to the Bison Books Edition
by Gregory A. Benford

UNIVERSITY OF NEBRASKA PRESS
LINCOLN AND LONDON

∞

First Bison Books printing: 1998

Library of Congress Cataloging-in-Publication Data
Verne, Jules, 1828–1905.
[Chasse au météore. English]
The chase of the golden meteor / by Jules Verne; introduction to the Bison Books edition by Gregory A. Benford.
p. cm.
"Illustrated."
ISBN 0-8032-9619-3 (pbk.: alk. paper)
I. Title.
PQ2469.C413 1998
843′.8—dc21
98-20801 CIP

Reprinted from the original 1909 edition by Grant Richards, London.

INTRODUCTION

THE EXACT DREAMER

Gregory Benford

If you've ever peered up into a night sky to glimpse the swiftly gliding white dot of an orbiting satellite, you've shared for a moment the wonder-world of Jules Verne. This handsome new edition of one of his last novels brings back the unique blend of good humor and child-like awe that made Verne the founder of modern, "hard" science fiction.

Why read about past wonders? Because, unlike yesterday's yellowing newspapers, the quality of true wonder fades quite slowly. Grand hopes speak out of our sense of adventure and possibility. Though we now have thousands of artificial satellites, the ideas and attitudes Verne packed into *The Chase of the Golden Meteor* are still alive today.

Verne invented modern science fiction. Others had written fantastic novels and stories, such as Mary Shelley's dark, brooding Gothic novel *Frankenstein*. But Verne devised *science* fiction—stories with the scientific content in the foreground, as much a character as any person.

We are living in his imagined, science-based world. More than any other figure of the nineteenth century, he saw the possibilities of the soaring century to come—and made things happen, by igniting the imaginations of people everywhere.

For decades he was the best known of all French authors, valued not so much for his plots but for his ideas. Because he wrote with a sense of wonder, he was regarded overseas as mostly a children's writer—but his work has outlasted vast numbers of "serious" novels about character and setting, which now seem like mere historical curiosities.

We can see why by looking at how this novel works its wonders. Verne labored hard to infuse his novels with the feeling that these events *could* happen, no matter how impossible they seemed at first glance.

He had great faith in the opening possibilities of the United States and often predicted that it would lead the world in the next century. Verne's amateur astronomers are from small-town USA. In his *From the Earth to the Moon* he had said, "The Yankees, the world's best mechanics, are engineers the way Italians are musicians and Germans are metaphysicians: by birth."

People with grand ideas are typical Verne heroes, feeling in their bones that by dreaming as exactly as possible they can live up to the full potential of their lives. This is his basic theme, lighting up over a hundred of his "extraordinary voyage" novels.

Verne had used Earth-orbiting rocks as plot motivators before, in his two Civil War–era novels about voyaging to the moon. By odd coincidence, this novel was published in the same year, 1908, that a large meteor (now thought to have been an icy cometary head) struck Siberia, devastating hundreds of square miles.

Verne's bolide is more benign. With his sure sense of pacing, plus antique terms (*aeroliths*), romantic subplots, and amusing asides ("unfortunately wives like this are rarely found outside novels"), he imbues the tale with narrative momentum.

Throughout Verne uses calculations, given to three or four significant figures, to give the tale an aura of reality. As usual, his men—this was long before women aspired to such things—were relentlessly practical. Grounding the tale in details is a technique he handed down to the countless big-book authors of today, who tell us how hotels or airports or battleships work, all in relentless, telling minutia.

In Verne we see the birth of hard science fiction (SF)—the variety that stays loyal to the facts, as nearly as the author knows them. Hard SF also sticks to the way engineers and scientists work. No lonely experimenters on mountaintops, inventing Frankensteins out of parts of dead bodies. No easy improvising around tough problems (well, some—particularly near the end). Verne's tinkerers work in groups, argue, make hard choices. Audiences of his time found such particulars gripping and convincing.

Still, he betrays an uncertain grasp of orbital mechanics, particularly exaggerating the power of a slight illumination from the ground to alter a satellite's orbit. A gold bolide is enormously unlikely, since ores are concentrated by water flows, and bringing an Earth-orbiting chunk from another planet would require improbable events. The gold's landing at terminal speed would have blown a crater about a mile across—indeed, at fifty-five yards across it is roughly the estimated size of the object that formed Meteor Crater in Arizona. Anyone standing "five hundred yards away" would have died instantly. Further, gold melts at slightly above a thousand degrees Fahrenheit, which means the bolide would have disintegrated in air; we now know that incoming rocks reach much higher temperatures. But Verne was doing the best he could with the astrophysics (a term not invented then) of his time.

To move the gold rock, a heroic inventor produces a totally new device, which of course works right away. The "neuter helicoidal current" is wholly imaginary physics, as are the "atomic howitzers." In the end, science prevents a crash in the gold market, and the marvelous machines cooked up at the last minute also pass into history, their secrets dying with their inventor.

Many writers were to follow in Verne's imaginative realist tradition, such as Arthur C. Clarke (*2001: A Space Odyssey*), Robert A. Heinlein, and of course, the other master SF writer of the nineteenth century, H. G. Wells.

Not that the technical agenda is the whole of the novel. There is an amused narrative voice, deliberately keeping matters light against a backdrop of astronomical scale. The Romeo and Juliet subplot and satirical asides about the role of money in the world seem a bit worn but still do their narrative duty.

His ending contrasts strongly with the expansive spirit Verne invokes in the rest of the narrative. His events explore the fantastic, then return the audience to their comfy world, the wonders banished. Such returns to the normal later became routine in filmed science fiction.

Verne died in 1905, only a few months before the Wright brothers' first flight at Kitty Hawk, South Carolina—but he had seen such flights in his mind's eye decades before, and the Wrights had read his novels. We can get a feeling for Verne's faith in the long-range possibilities of humanity from the remarkable memorial his son placed over his grave. It shows Verne with hair streaming, as if he is in flight, breaking free of his shroud and tomb, rising up magnificently from the dead. Above it are simply his name and the words *Onward to immortality and eternal youth*. It's hard to be more optimistic than that.

Hard SF is often optimistic, but not unsophisticated. Verne foresaw many bleak aspects of our century as well—total war, industrial squalor, social dislocations. Indeed, an early, bleak vision of our time went unpublished because nobody wanted to hear that prospect.

But beyond the inevitable troubles he always saw fresh possibility looming ahead. Many of his inventions "came true" because Verne was often extrapolating from ideas already present in the scientific or engineering community, but he always took them further. Even as a struggling writer, he showed his intention to work this way. In 1856 he wrote in his journal, thinking about his ambitions, "Not mere poetry, but analytic fantasy. Something monomaniacal. Things playing a more important part than people, love giving way to deduction and other sources of ideas, style, subject, interest. The basis of the novel transferred from the heart to the head."

And what dreams Verne had! We can grasp how much he changed the world by recalling real events that appeared first as acts of imagination in his novels. The American submarine *Nautilus*, its name taken from *20,000 Leagues Under the Sea*, surfaced at the North Pole and talked by radio with the president of the United States, less than a century after the novel was published. The explorer Haroun Tazieff, a Verne fan who had read *Journey to the Center of the Earth*, climbed down into the rumbling throat of a volcano in Africa, seeking secrets of the earth's core. An Italian adventurer coasted over the icy Arctic wastes in a dirigible, just as Verne proposed. A French explorer crawled into the caves of southern Europe, stumbling upon the ancient campgrounds of early humans, standing before underground lakes where mammoths once roasted over crackling fires—as Verne had envisioned. In 1877 Verne foresaw a journey through the entire solar system, a feat accomplished by NASA's robot voyagers a century later. He excited not merely a generation but a century.

His attention to detail, balanced against his soaring imagination, makes the book in your hands still exciting.

CONTENTS

LIST OF ILLUSTRATIONS

Judge Proth in his garden

I

In which Judge Proth performs one of the most agreeable duties of his office before returning to his garden.

THERE is no reason for hiding from the reader that the town in which this singular story commences is situated in Virginia, United States of America. With his permission, we will call this town Whaston, and we will place it in the east, on the right bank of the river Potomac; but we deem it useless to specify the exact whereabouts of Whaston, which does not appear even on the best maps.

On the 12th of March, in the year our story opens, the inhabitants of Whaston that happened to be walking along Exeter Street, after their breakfast, had the pleasure of seeing a horseman ride up the street slowly and then down the steep incline at the same prudent pace, after which performance he stopped on Constitution Square, situated almost in the centre of the town.

This horseman, who was of pure Yankee type—a type having its own distinction—could not be more than thirty. He was over the medium height, had a fine, healthy complexion, regular features, brown hair, lightening to chestnut in his pointed beard, which made his face, with its clean-shaven lips, seem longer. A flowing cloak covered him to the legs, and fell with ample curve over the horse's croup. He managed his somewhat mettlesome steed with equal skill and firmness. Everything in his attitude indicated a man of action, decision, and impulse—a man who would never vacillate between desire and fear, as hesitating characters do. His outwardly cool demeanour did not altogether hide his natural impatience.

Since the horseman was a stranger to the town, those who saw him for the first time might well wonder what was the object of his visit, and whether he were simply passing through their midst or were intending to sojourn among them. If he were seeking an hotel, there were plenty to choose from. In fact, in no other centre of the United States, or elsewhere, could a traveller find better attendance, better accommodation, and better food at moderate prices. It is really unfortunate that a town provided with such advantages should not figure on the maps.

Apparently, the stranger had no intention of remaining at Whaston; so that the hotel-keepers' smiles of invitation would be lost on him. Indifferent to everything around him, he absent-mindedly rode round the Square without even suspecting that he was exciting public curiosity, and yet the curiosity was manifest enough. As soon as he was noticed, a running fire of questions and answers was exchanged on the various doorsteps between masters or servants.

"Which way did he come?"

"Along Exeter Street."

"And where did he come from?"

"From Wilcox suburb, it would seem."

"He's been riding round the Square for half an hour or so."

"No doubt he's waiting for somebody."

"I guess so. And he looks a bit impatient."

"It's up Exeter Street he keeps looking."

"That's the way they'll come."

"Who? He or she?"

"How do I know? . . . Anyway, he's smart enough."

"Then, he has an appointment, perhaps."

"Yes, an appointment, but not of the kind you mean."

"How do you know?"

"Don't you see that he has stopped three times in front of Mr. Proth's door. . . ."

"And, as Mr. John Proth is judge in Whaston..."

"You've hit it. He must have got a lawsuit."

"And his opponent is late."

"You are right."

"Judge Proth will soon make matters up between 'em."

"He's a clever fellow."

"And a good one, too."

The foregoing conversation did not appear to be far wrong, for the traveller had several times pulled up his horse opposite the judge's house. He glanced at the door, he glanced at the windows, then he remained motionless, as if expecting some one would come out. But soon, his horse growing restless, he was obliged to start off again. At last, however, just as he drew rein once more, the door opened wide, and a man showed himself on the steps descending to the footpath.

The stranger immediately accosted him.

"Mr. John Proth, I presume?" he said, raising his hat.

"Right you are," replied the judge.

"Just one question, requiring a yes or a no from you."

"Ask it, sir."

"Has any one been here this morning inquiring for Mr. Seth Stanfort?"

"Not that I am aware."

"Thank you."

Having pronounced these last words, and raised his hat a second time, the horseman rode off, and turned up Exeter Street again.

Now the general opinion was that the unknown horseman must have business with the judge. Most likely he himself was Seth Stanfort, who had arrived first at the rendezvous. The question at present to be settled was whether the hour of the appointment were past and the traveller were definitely quitting the town.

As we are in America, among the nation that of all others is fondest of betting, it is not astonishing that wagers ranging from half a dollar up to five and six hundred—not more—were laid on the chances of the stranger's return, by some of the employees of hotels on the Square and by certain inquisitive pedestrians.

Meanwhile, Judge Proth had contented himself with gazing after the retreating figure of his late visitor. The judge was a wise magistrate, and a philosopher to boot, whose fifty years might all count as years of wisdom, since he was born wise. Moreover, being a bachelor—a proof of his wisdom—his life had never been troubled by anxiety and stress, an exemption highly favourable to the practice of philosophy. Having been born at Whaston, he had hardly ever left the place, and was both respected and loved by his townsmen, who knew he cared little for life's ambitions.

In all his actions he was guided by the sense of justice. To foibles and sometimes to faults in others he showed himself indulgent. His aim was always to arrange the disputes that were brought before him, to reconcile adversaries, to smooth over difficulties, to make matters go easily, and to soften the shocks inevitable in every social organization. The judge was fairly wealthy. If he exercised the magisterial office, it was rather from taste ; and he had no intention or desire of mounting to higher dignities. He was fond of tranquillity both for himself and others. He considered men as neighbours in existence with whom it was one's interest to be on good terms. It was 'early to bed and early to rise' with him. If he read a few favourite authors of the old and new world, he confined himself, for the rest, to a steady-going local paper, *The Whaston News*, in which advertisements were more prominent than politics. Every day he took his constitutional walk for an hour or two, when the number of hats that were raised to him, and the number of times he raised his own, had effects that obliged him to renew his headgear about every three months. Save for these walks and the hours outside devoted to his profession, he stayed in his peaceful and comfortable dwelling, cultivating his garden flowers, which rewarded him for his assiduity by charming him with their fresh colours and lavishing on him their suave perfumes.

From this brief character sketch it may be understood that Mr. John Proth thought no more about the question asked by the stranger. If the latter, instead of applying to the master of the house, had made inquiries from the old servant Kate, she would probably have wanted to know what she must say if any one came to the judge's to see Mr. Seth Stanfort; nor would she have refrained from trying to find out whether the stranger intended to return in the morning or the afternoon.

Mr. Proth would have disdained such inquisitiveness, excusable in his servant since she belonged to the feminine sex. He did not even remark the mild excitement aroused in the street; and, after shutting his door, returned to water his roses, lilies, geraniums, and mignonette. The inquisitives of the town did not imitate his discretion, and continued their observation.

The horseman rode up Exeter Street and reached its farther extremity, which commanded the west side of the town. Entering here the Wilcox suburb above-mentioned, he checked his steed, and, without dismounting, began to look around him. From this vantage-point he was able to perceive the whole of the environs within a mile's radius, and to see right down the road before him that zigzagged for three miles along to the country town of Steel, whose steeples were visible across the Potomac on the verge of the horizon. Apparently he did not discover what he was seeking, and manifested his impatience by a series of nervous gestures, which influenced the horse in turn, so that the animal's restiveness had to be restrained.

Ten minutes elapsed; then the stranger, returning down Exeter Street, came into the Square for the fifth time.

"After all," he said to himself, as he consulted his watch, "she's not late. The appointment was fixed for seven minutes past ten, and it's only just half-past nine. . . . The distance from Steel to Whaston, which she has to do, is the same as that from Brial to Whaston, which I have done, and can be covered in less than twenty minutes. . . . The road is a good one, the weather is dry, and, so far as I know, the bridge hasn't been carried away by a flood. . . . There is, therefore, neither hindrance nor obstacle. . . . Under these circumstances, if she fails to keep the appointment, the failure will be intentional. . . . However, punctuality consists in arriving just in the nick of time, not in anticipating the hour. In reality, it is I who am to blame, since I have arrived sooner than a methodical man should. . . . It is true that politeness, not to speak of any other sentiment, required that I should be first at the rendezvous."

This monologue was pursued while the horseman was retracing his steps down Exeter Street, and was concluded just as the steed's hoofs resounded once more on the macadamized Square. Those who had wagered on the stranger's return gained their bet. Consequently, when they saw man and horse pass by the hotels, they smiled encouragingly, whereas the losers shrugged their shoulders.

At last the town clock struck ten. Stopping his horse, the stranger counted the strokes, and ascertained that the clock was right by his watch. Seven minutes, and the hour of the appointment would have come and gone by. Seth Stanfort took up his position at the entrance to Exeter Street. It was evident that neither he nor his steed could remain still. At the moment plenty of people were abroad. To those who were going up the street he paid not the slightest attention. But on all who were descending he flashed an eager glance—or rather on all who were riding or driving, for the person he was expecting would not be on foot.

Three minutes were now wanting to bring the hand to the seventh dot, just the time required for a vehicle and horse to do the distance sharply; yet there was no sign of one or the other at the top of the hill, nor even of bicycle or motor-car, which last might have rushed down with sixty seconds or so to spare.

Seth Stanfort shot a final glance up the street. His eyes sparkled ominously, and he murmured in a most decided tone:

"If she isn't here at seven past ten, I won't marry."

As if in response to this declaration, the gallop of a horse was heard at the top of the hill. The animal, which was a fine creature, was ridden by a young woman, who guided him with equal grace and dexterity. The pedestrians at once cleared out of the way, leaving a free course down to the Square. Seth Stanfort recognized the person he was waiting for, and his face resumed its impassible expression. Without further word or gesture, he set his horse in motion, and proceeded quietly to the judge's house.

The inquisitives were on the alert, and drew near, but the stranger was not in the smallest degree concerned. A few seconds later, the lady rider was in the Square also, and her steed, white with foam, was reined in two yards from the judge's door. The stranger took off his hat and said :

" How do you do, Miss Walker ? "

" How do you do, Mr. Stanfort ? " the lady answered, making a charming bow.

With bated breath the witnesses of this scene continued their comments.

" If they have a lawsuit, the best thing would be to settle it amicably."

" Oh ! Mr. Proth will bring 'em to that."

" And, if they aren't married, they might do worse than arrange their difference with a wedding."

Perhaps these remarks did not reach the ears of the couple. At any rate, each of them seemed to be perfectly oblivious of the curiosity they had awakened. Seth Stanfort was preparing to get off his horse, when the judge's door opened afresh, and Mr. Proth appeared on the threshold, with the old servant behind him. They had heard the pawing and stamping of the two animals' hoofs, and the former had quitted his garden, the latter her kitchen. At present both were willing to investigate.

Instead of dismounting, the gentleman visitor spoke from the saddle, and said to the magistrate :

"Judge Proth, I am Mr. Seth Stanfort, of Boston, Massachusetts."

"I am happy to get acquainted with you, Mr. Stanfort," replied the judge.

"And this lady is Miss Arcadia Walker, of Trenton, New Jersey," continued the visitor.

"I esteem it an honour to be introduced to you, Miss Walker," added the judge, with his eyes bent critically on the figure of the horsewoman.

Miss Arcadia Walker was an attractive damsel, twenty-four years of age. Her eyes were of pale blue, her hair dark chestnut ; her fresh complexion was just tinted a little by exposure to the open air. Her teeth were white and perfectly regular ; her height was more than the average ; her shape beautifully proportioned, and her bearing lithe and elegant. Not at all hampered by her riding dress, she sat her horse easily, despite the restiveness which the animal displayed in sympathy with that of Seth Stanfort's steed. Her gloved hands toyed with the reins, and a connoisseur would have had no difficulty in pronouncing on her skill as a rider. In all her person there was ample evidence of her belonging to what might be called the American aristocracy, were it not that this epithet is not consonant with the democratic instincts of the New World.

Miss Arcadia Walker, who had been born in New Jersey, was without relatives other than distant ones. Being free to do as she willed, since she had an independent fortune, she led a life in agreement with her tastes. Already an experienced traveller, and having been in the principal countries of Europe, she knew what was being said and done in London, Paris, Berlin, Vienna, and Rome; and of what she had learnt in her numerous peregrinations she could talk with the natives of these countries in their own language. Her education, superintended by a guardian who was now dead, had been most thoroughly provided for. Even the practice of business was not unfamiliar to her, and in the management of her fortune she exhibited remarkable shrewdness.

What has just been said of Miss Arcadia Walker might have been asserted with equal truth about Mr. Seth Stanfort. Free also, rich also, and also fond of travelling, he had journeyed all over the world, and was scarcely ever in his native town of Boston. In winter he was to be found in the old continent, and in the chief capitals of the world, where he had often met his adventurous fellow-countrywoman. In summer he returned to the States and the seaside places frequented by opulent American families. There, too, Miss Arcadia Walker and he had likewise met.

Similar tastes had gradually brought these two young, valiant persons into nearer relations; and, as both of them were equally eager to go wherever war or politics were arousing public attention, it was not astonishing that they should have ultimately come to the resolution of uniting their lives, without changing their habits. They would be no longer acting like two sea-craft navigating together, but like one larger and better-rigged vessel thoroughly equipped for sailing over all the seas of the globe.

It was not, therefore, a lawsuit which had induced them to present themselves before the Judge of Whaston. No. After complying with the legal formalities required in Massachusetts and New Jersey, they had agreed to be at Judge Proth's on the 12th of March, at seven minutes past ten, to perform what amateurs regard as being the most important act in human life.

As soon as the two parties had duly introduced themselves to the magistrate, the latter was under the necessity of asking their business.

"I wish to make Miss Arcadia Walker my wife," answered the gentleman.

"And I wish to make Mr. Seth Stanfort my husband," echoed the lady.

The judge bowed and said:

"I am at your service, Mr. Stanfort, and at yours too, Miss Walker."

The visitors bowed in turn.

"When will it suit you to have the marriage performed?" continued Mr. Proth.

"At once, if you are at liberty," replied Seth Stanfort.

"We shall be leaving Whaston directly after the ceremony," added Miss Walker.

The judge's attitude indicated how much he regretted, and all the city with him, not being able to retain at Whaston this charming couple that honoured the place by their presence.

"I am quite ready," he said, stepping back, in order that the doorway might be less encumbered.

Seth Stanfort put up his hand.

"Is it really necessary," he asked, "that Miss Arcadia and I should dismount?"

Mr. Proth reflected for a moment.

"No," he said. "The marriage can quite well be celebrated on horseback."

It would have been difficult to come across a more accommodating official than the judge, even in America.

"In the name of the law, . . . I declare you joined in matrimony"

" One question only I must put," Mr. Proth added. " Are all the legal formalities complied with ? "

" They are," answered the bridegroom.

And he held out to the magistrate a duplicate licence made out in due form by the proper authorities of Boston and Trenton, after payment of the fees. Mr. Proth took the papers, and attentively through his gold-rimmed spectacles read them from beginning to end.

" The documents are in order," he pronounced, " and I will deliver you the marriage certificate."

At present the inquisitives of the Square had come quite close to the horses, impromptu witnesses of this original wedding. Mr. Proth went up the lower steps of his perron, and, loud enough to be heard by principals and accessories, he said :

" Mr. Seth Stanfort, will you take Miss Arcadia Walker as your wedded wife ? "

" I will."

" Miss Arcadia Walker, will you take Mr. Seth Stanfort as your wedded husband ? "

" I will."

The magistrate kept silence for a few seconds, then, as serious as a photographer coming to the critical moment of his operation, he uttered the words :

" In the name of the law, Mr. Seth Stanfort of Boston, and Miss Arcadia Walker of Trenton, I declare you joined in matrimony."

The bride and bridegroom approached each other and clasped hands, as if to seal the act they had just accomplished. Then each presented the judge with a five hundred dollar note.

"Your fees," said Seth Stanfort.

"For the poor," added Mrs. Arcadia Stanfort.

And the two, after bowing to the judge, shook the reins of their horses and rode off rapidly in the direction of Wilcox suburb.

"Well I never! Well I never! . . ." exclaimed Kate, recovering from her ten minutes' surprise and loss of speech.

"What's the matter, Kate?" questioned Mr. Proth.

Old Kate dropped the corner of her apron, which she had been twisting into a rope.

"My opinion is, Judge," she said, "that those two young folks are mad."

"Perhaps! perhaps! Kate," acquiesced Mr. Proth, while seizing his watering-can. "But it's nothing to be astonished at. People that get married are generally a trifle mad."

II

Which introduces the reader into the house of Dean Forsyth, and acquaints him with the latter's nephew, Francis Gordon, and the servant, Mitz.

"MITZ! . . . Mitz! . . ."

"Sonny? . . ."

"What's Uncle Dean got?"

"I dunno."

"Is he ill?"

"Not a bit! But if the thing goes on, he will be, and sure."

These questions and answers were exchanged between a young man twenty-three years of age and a woman of sixty-five, in the dining-room of a house in Elizabeth Street, situated in the same town of Whaston where the marriage related in the preceding chapter had recently been performed.

This Elizabeth Street house belonged to Mr. Dean Forsyth, a gentleman of forty-five, who looked his age. He had a big head with a thick touzle of hair, small eyes protected by high-power spectacles, stooping shoulders, a puissant neck, enwrapped in all seasons with two folds of necktie reaching up to his chin; he wore a loose, crumpled frock-coat, a sleazy waistcoat whose lower buttons were never fastened, trousers that scarcely came down to his over-sized shoes, a tasselled skull-cap on his grey hair; add to this a face wrinkled everywhere and adorned with a bit of beard on his chin, a temper always on the point of exploding; and some idea is afforded of the person about whom Francis Gordon and Mitz were talking on the morning of the 21st of March.

Francis Gordon, who had lost his parents when a child, had been brought up by Mr. Dean Forsyth, his mother's brother. Although the heir to his uncle's fortune, which was considerable, he had, none the less, with Mr. Forsyth's approval, chosen a profession. After taking a degree at Harvard, he had qualified as a barrister, and was now practising at Whaston, where the widow, the orphan, and property rights had no more ardent defender. He was familiar with law and jurisprudence, and spoke with ease and eloquence. All his colleagues, young and old, esteemed him, and so far he had not made an enemy. He was handsome, had fine chestnut hair, beautiful black eyes, distinguished manners; was obliging without ostentation, witty without malice, and acquitted himself creditably in outdoor sports and games. It was consequently natural he should be classed among the eligible young men of the town, natural, too, that he should pretend to the hand of the winsome Jenny Hudelson, daughter of Doctor Hudelson and his wife *née* Flora Clarish.

However, it is too soon to call the reader's attention to this young lady. It will be more fitting for her to make her appearance in the midst of her family, and the opportunity has not yet arrived. There will not be long to wait. But a rigorous method must be observed in this story, which necessitates extreme precision.

As for Francis Gordon, we may add that he lived in the Elizabeth Street house, and did not intend to quit it until the day of his marriage with Miss Jenny. Having explained thus much, we will leave Miss Jenny Hudelson in her own home, and proceed to say that Mitz was the confidant of her master's nephew, and that she had the same affection for him she would have had for a son, or rather a grandson, since grandmothers generally excel in maternal tenderness.

Mitz, who was a model servant, and whose like it would be hard to find nowadays, belonged to that species of domestics in which something of the dog and something of the cat coexist. She was attached to her masters and she was attached to the house. As may easily be imagined, Mitz never failed to speak her mind to Mr. Dean Forsyth. When he was in the wrong, she told him so plainly, and in extravagant language, which had to be heard in order to be appreciated. If he would not plead guilty, one thing only remained to him, to take refuge in his study and lock himself in.

Not that the den was such a lonely place. He was sure of always finding some one else there, who, like himself, used to slip away from Mitz's remonstrances and lectures. This other occupant was called Omicron, on account of his diminutive stature. Having at the age of fifteen attained the height of four feet six, he stopped growing any more! His real name was Tom Wife, and his age at present was over fifty. For thirty-five years he had been in the same service, his first master being the father of Francis Gordon's uncle. However, his duties under the government of the second generation were of a more elevated character. He helped Mr. Dean Forsyth in certain labours which that gentleman carried on with great enthusiasm and assiduity; and, a thing worthy to be noted, displayed a zeal therein equal to that of his employer.

And what was Mr. Forsyth's occupation? Medicine, law, literature, art, business? No, none of these. Sciences? Well, not sciences in the plural, but science in the singular, a science in particular; the sublime pursuit of astronomy.

Mr. Dean Forsyth was entirely taken up with the investigation of planets and stars. But little of that which happened on the surface of our globe seemed to interest him. He was always living in the infinite. Still, as he would not have been able, if he tried, to lunch or dine in these ethereal regions, he was compelled, at least twice a day, to descend into the mundane sphere. It so happened that, on the morning of the 21st of March, he was a long time in descending, which caused Mitz to grumble as she wandered round the table.

" Isn't he going to come at all ? " she muttered.

" Is Omicron up with him ? " asked Francis.

" He's sure to be where his master is," replied the servant. " Any way, I haven't legs enough " —such was the estimable Mitz's expression—" to climb up to his perch ! "

The perch in question was neither more nor less than a tower, the top balcony of which rose some twenty feet above the roof of the house—an observatory, to give it its true name. Below the balcony was a circular room pierced with four windows that faced the four cardinal points. Inside were several telescopes set on revolving stands, and provided with lenses of considerable power, which did not rust for want of use. The only thing to be feared was that Mr. Dean Forsyth and Omicron might wear out their eyes by dint of looking into their instruments.

They both spent most of their days and nights in this room, relieving each other, it is true. They gazed, observed, peered into the starry depths, upheld by the hope of making some discovery to which the name of Dean Forsyth might be attached. When the sky was serene, they were pretty content. But, unfortunately, northward of the thirty-seventh parallel traversing the State of Virginia, the sky was not always serene. There were clouds, mists, and haloes more frequently than master and servitor desired. And many were the objurgations and anathemas hurled against the firmament across which the winds trailed their ragged vapours.

During the second half of this month of March Mr. Dean Forsyth's patience had been more tried than ever. For some days the sky had continued cloudy, to the great despair of the astronomer. On the 21st a strong west wind swept wave after wave of dense, low-hanging mist athwart his field of vision.

"What a nuisance!" sighed Mr. Dean Forsyth for the tenth time, after a last fruitless attempt to see. "I have a presentiment that we are losing a unique opportunity, that we are allowing a sensational discovery to go by."

"It's very possible," answered Omicron. "It's very probable even; for, a few days ago, when the sky was a little clearer, I thought I perceived . . ."

"And I too saw, Omicron."

"Both of us, then, both of us at the same time!"

"Omicron!" protested Mr. Dean Forsyth.

"Yes! you, first, no doubt," acquiesced Omicron,

MANY WERE THE OBJURGATIONS AND ANATHEMAS HURLED AGAINST THE FIRMAMENT

shaking his head significantly. "But when I thought I perceived the thing in question, it seemed to me to be . . ."

"And I," interrupted the astronomer, "I am sure it must have been a meteor travelling from north to south."

"Yes, Mr. Dean, perpendicular to the sun's direction.

"To its apparent direction, Omicron."

"Apparent, of course."

"And it was the 16th of this month."

"The 16th."

"At thirty-seven minutes, twenty seconds past seven."

"Twenty seconds," repeated Omicron, "as I noticed by our clock."

"And it has not reappeared since!" cried Mr. Dean Forsyth, stretching out a threatening hand towards the sky.

"How could it? Clouds! . . . clouds! . . . clouds! . . . For the last five days not enough blue in the sky to make a handkerchief of!"

"One would think," exclaimed the astronomer, stamping his foot, "it was done on purpose. I do believe such things happen only to me."

"To us," corrected Omicron, who looked upon himself as having an equal share in all that concerned his master.

In reality, the inhabitants of the district had just as much reason to complain of clouds darkening the sky. Whether the sun shines or not is a matter that affects every one.

But however general might be the reason for complaint, no one certainly could have pretended to be in such bad humour as Mr. Dean Forsyth when the town was enshrouded with one of those fogs against which the most powerful telescopes are of no use. Such fogs were not rare at Whaston, although situated on the banks of the limpid Potomac and not on the muddy Thames.

And what was the phenomenon that master and servant had perceived, or had believed they perceived, on the 16th of March, when the sky was clear? Nothing less than a bolide of spherical form travelling from north to south with extreme swiftness, and so bright that it rivalled with the more diffused light of the sun. Yet, as its distance from the earth must have measured a considerable number of miles, its flight might have been followed, in spite of its speed, for a fairly long time, if the unlucky fog had not interfered to prevent all observation.

Since that moment the astronomer had hardly ceased harping on the chance he had missed. Would the bolide return to the horizon of Whaston? Would it be possible to calculate the bolide's elements, mass, weight, and nature? Would not some other astronomer more favoured than himself discover its passage in some different region of the sky? Would he, Dean Forsyth, be justified in attributing this discovery to himself, and to give his own name to the bolide, which he had seen so little of? Would not all the honour rather fall to one or another savant of the old or new world that spent his life in investigating space by night and by day?

"Monopolizers!" protested Mr. Dean Forsyth. "Sky-pirates!"

During the whole of this morning of the 21st of March, neither the astronomer nor Omicron had been able to make up their minds, notwithstanding the bad weather, to quit the window looking towards the north. And their wrath had grown in proportion as the hours glided by. Now they had ceased to speak. Dean Forsyth's eyes wandered along the vast horizon bounded on the hither side by the fantastic profile of the Serbor hills, above which a fresh breeze was chasing the greyish mist. Omicron was standing on tiptoe to get a better view than his natural height afforded. The astronomer had folded his arms, and his clenched fists were pressed against his chest. The servant with his bent fingers was clutching at the window-sill. A few birds were flying by, with sharp, short cries, seeming to mock the two biped creatures forced thus to remain on the surface of the ground. Ah! if only the bipeds could have followed these birds in their flight, they would have traversed the mist in a twinkling, and then perhaps have perceived the asteroid continuing its course in the dazzling sun's light!

At this instant some one knocked at the door. Dean Forsyth and Omicron, who were lost in contemplation, heard nothing. The door opened, and Francis Gordon showed himself on the threshold. Neither of the occupants of the room turned round. The nephew went up to the uncle and touched him lightly on the arm. Mr. Dean Forsyth let fall on his nephew such a far-away look that it might have come from Sirius, or at least from the moon.

"What is it?" he asked.

"Lunch is waiting, uncle."

"Ah! dear me! so lunch is waiting! We are waiting too!"

"What are you waiting for?"

"The sun," put in Omicron, whose answer was approved by a nod from his master.

"But you haven't invited the sun to lunch, I believe. We can sit down to table without the sun."

What reply could be made to this pertinent remark? If the greater light refused to exhibit its rays throughout the day, was Mr. Dean Forsyth to persist in fasting till evening? It almost seemed as though such was his intention, for he made no movement indicative of compliance with his nephew's invitation.

"Uncle," urged Francis, "Mitz is getting impatient."

At once the astronomer became conscious of reality. He was only too well acquainted with Mitz's impatience and its consequences. Since the messenger had been despatched by her, the situation was a grave one, and he must delay no longer.

"What time is it?" he asked.

"Forty-six minutes past eleven," answered Francis.

This was indeed the hour by the clock, whereas, usually, the uncle and nephew sat down opposite each other at eleven o'clock to the second.

"Forty-six minutes past eleven!" repeated the astronomer, pretending to be angry, in order to hide his own fears. "I cannot understand Mitz's being so unpunctual."

"But, uncle," said Francis, "it's the third time we have knocked at the door."

Without a word more Mr. Dean Forsyth descended the stairs, while Omicron, who generally waited at table, stayed on guard, watching for the sun's return. Uncle and nephew entered the dining-room. Mitz was there. She stared at her master, and he hung down his head.

"And *My Crown?*" she questioned, this being her pronunciation of Omicron's name.

"He is engaged upstairs," replied Francis. "We will manage without him this morning."

"All the better," grumbled Mitz. "I wish he'd stay and moon in his *hobservandtory* for good and all. I shouldn't miss him."

The lunch began, and for a while eating replaced conversation. Mitz, who was accustomed to talk when bringing in the dishes and changing the plates, did not open her mouth. The silence at last grew irksome, and Francis, desirous to produce a diversion, asked:

"Are you content with your morning, uncle?"

"No," said the latter; "the sky was not propitious, and to-day, in particular, I am annoyed there should be no sun."

"Are you on the verge of some fresh astronomic discovery?"

"I think so, Francis. But I can't be sure until a fresh observation . . ."

"That's what you've been at, then, for the last week," interrupted Mitz grimly, "getting up even in the middle of the night. Yes! I heard you three times last night. Thank God, *I ain't lost my eyes*," she added, in response to her master's gesture of protest, and to let him know perhaps that she wasn't deaf.

"You are right, my good Mitz," said Mr. Dean Forsyth, in a conciliatory tone, which was thrown away upon her.

"An *astrocomic* discovery!" the worthy Mitz continued. "And when you have worn yourself to fiddlestrings with poking your head into your tubes, and caught *brown chitis* or some other fine malady, you'll be in a mess that your stars won't get you out of, unless the doctor makes you swallow 'em as pills."

Convinced that he would come off second best in this sort of dialogue, the astronomer deemed it more profitable not to retort. He therefore went on with his meal in silence, but embarrassed to the point of confusing his glass with his serviette.

Francis endeavoured to make his uncle talk, but the latter did not appear to hear what he said. Only when, in despair, he made a commonplace remark on the weather, did Mr. Dean Forsyth raise his head. At the same instant a thicker cloud, passing, cast its shadow into the dining-room. Glancing through the window, and letting his fork drop on the table, the astronomer cried:

"Hang it! why can't the rain come down and rid the heavens of these confounded black vapours!"

"Sakes!" said Mitz, "after three weeks' drought, it would be welcome, if only for the ground."

"The ground! . . . the ground! . . ." murmured Mr. Dean Forsyth with such contempt that the old servant added:

"Yes, the ground, sir. Seems to me it's worth the sky from which you are never willing to descend . . . even at lunch-time!"

"Come, Mitz . . ." said Francis coaxingly.

But Mitz wasn't to be coaxed.

"I don't want wheedling," she continued in the same tone, "and it ain't much good staring at the moon till you're moithered, if you don't know it's bound to rain in spring. If it can't rain in the month o' March, when will it rain, I wonder?"

"Uncle," approved Francis, "it's true we are in March, at the commencement of spring. We must have patience. Soon it will be summer; and the sky will be blue. You will be able to carry on your work under better conditions. Have patience, uncle!"

"Patience, Francis!" answered the astronomer, whose forehead was as sombre as the atmosphere; "patience! . . . And suppose it goes away so far that we shan't be able to see it? . . . Suppose it shouldn't appear again above the horizon?"

"It? . . . What it?" asked Mitz.

At this instant Omicron's voice was heard:

"Sir! . . . Sir! . . ."

"Something fresh!" cried Mr. Dean Forsyth, pushing his chair back quickly and rushing towards the door.

Hardly had he reached it when a bright ray shot through the window, making the glasses and bottles sparkle that were on the table.

"The sun! . . . the sun! . . ." repeated the astronomer, as he ran upstairs.

"Lawks-a-mercy!" said Mitz, sitting down

"THE SUN! . . . THE SUN! . . ." REPEATED THE ASTRONOMER AS HE RAN UPSTAIRS

on a chair. "There he is, gone to shut himself up with *My Crown* in the *hobservandtory.* You may call him now till you're black i' the face. As for lunch, it'll have to eat itself, I suppose, unless them blessed stars come and take it up to him!"

Thus expressed herself Mitz, unheard by her master, who had just entered the observatory, very much out of breath. The south-west wind had freshened and chased the clouds in the direction of the east. Right up to the zenith, a break showed all that part of the sky in which the meteor had been observed. The room was flooded with the sun's beams.

"Well? . . ." questioned Mr. Dean Forsyth, "What have you found?"

"The sun," answered Omicron. "But it won't be for long. Already in the west there are some new clouds forming."

"Then, there's not a minute to lose!" exclaimed the astronomer, fixing his telescope, while the servant did the same with a smaller instrument of the same kind. For nearly three-quarters of an hour they adjusted and readjusted their lenses, and patiently searched every nook and corner of the celestial sphere within their range. They had calculated the exact right ascension and declination at which the bolide appeared to them in the first instance, passing subsequently across the Whaston zenith. Of this they were sure. Yet in this region there was nothing to be seen. Throughout the space which offered such an opportunity for a meteoric promenade there was no trace of the asteroid.

"Nothing!" pronounced Mr. Dean Forsyth, wiping his reddened eyes.

"Nothing!" echoed Omicron, in a plaintive tone.

It was too late to exhaust themselves in further efforts. The clouds were returning, the sky was growing gloomy again. The glimpse of sunshine had departed for the day. Soon there remained nought but a uniform mass of grey dingy vapour everywhere, out of which began to fall a drizzling rain. Both master and servant were in despair. They were compelled to abandon their watch.

"And yet," said Omicron, "we are quite sure we saw it."

"Sure!" cried Mr. Dean Forsyth, raising his arms aloft, and in a tone betraying both anxiety and jealousy, he added: "We are only too sure. For others may have seen it as well as ourselves. . . . If only we could have prevented them! . . . and him too. . . . Sydney Hudelson!"

III

In which something is said about Dr. Sydney Hudelson, his wife, Mrs. Flora Hudelson, and Miss Jenny and Miss Loo, their daughters.

"IF only that intriguing Forsyth didn't see it!" These words were spoken by Dr. Sydney Hudelson himself, and to himself, on the 21st of March, as he stood in his sanctum.

He was a doctor of medicine, but did not practise at Whaston, preferring to devote his time and intelligence to vaster and more sublime speculations. An intimate friend of Dean Forsyth's, he was, none the less, his rival. Taken up with the same hobby, he had, like him, no eyes save for the broad welkin, and, like his friend also, he devoted his mind solely to the solution of the astronomic enigmas of the universe.

Doctor Hudelson had large means, both in his personal right and through his wife, whose maiden name was Flora Clarish. Having been prudently husbanded, this double fortune made ample provision for the doctor's own future and that of his two daughters, Jenny and Loo, whose respective ages at present were eighteen and fourteen. As for the head of the family's years, they numbered forty and seven, though the baldness of his cranium made him appear older.

The astronomic rivalry that existed in a latent state between the doctor and Mr. Dean Forsyth was not without some slight disturbing influence on the relations of the two families, which, however, remained very united. While they did not quarrel about planets and stars already discovered by somebody or other, they often discussed on their meteorological or astronomical observations, and drifted into disputes of somewhat acrimonious character. Had there been a Mrs. Forsyth, the consequences might have been serious. But Mr. Dean's inveterate bachelorhood facilitated reconciliations, there being one person less to appease.

True, there was Mrs. Flora. She, however, was an excellent wife, mother, and mistress, by nature very peaceable, incapable of backbiting, and not, as so many ladies in the old and new world, in the habit of lunching on slanders and dining on calumny. Curious to say, this model spouse strove to calm her husband when he came home excited after arguing with his intimate crony Forsyth. And, what was stranger still, Mrs. Hudelson was quite content for her husband to busy himself with astronomy, on condition he returned from the azure of the firmament whenever he was invited to do so. Unlike Mitz with Mr. Forsyth, she did not harass her other half. She put up with his lateness at meals. She did not fume and rage when he forgot the hour, and contrived to keep the plates hot and the meat from burning. She even inquired after his work, and her kindly heart dictated encouraging language to her when the astronomer seemed to have lost his way in the starry wilds. She was a woman of the sort we could wish every husband to have married, and especially astronomers. Unfortunately, her species is rarely met with outside novels.

Her elder daughter Jenny seemed likely to follow in her mother's steps along the path of life. Evidently Francis Gordon, Jenny Hudelson's future husband, was destined to become the happiest of men. It would have been hard to discover throughout the States a girl of greater attractions and qualities, be this said without disparagement of other American girls. Jenny was of fair complexion, with blue eyes, pink cheeks, pretty hands and feet and waist; and had as much grace and modesty as she had goodness and intelligence. Consequently, Francis appreciated her just as much as she appreciated him. Moreover, Mr. Dean Forsyth's nephew, possessing the esteem of the Hudelson family, had been most favourably received when he asked Jenny's hand in marriage. The two young people suited each other very well. Jenny's character and domestic aptitudes were all that could be wished for in a household, and Francis had the prospect of his uncle's fortune. For the moment, however, there was no need to think of inheritances. The present offered quite sufficient guarantees. The marriage was to be celebrated shortly by the Reverend Mr. O'Garth of Saint Andrew's, the principal church in this fine town of Whaston.

There would certainly be a great many people at the ceremony, for the two families were held in high esteem; and, on the wedding-day, little Loo, gayest of the gay, would be her sister's first bridesmaid. Loo, being not yet fifteen, had a right to be gay. She was the embodiment of perpetual motion, and was roguish enough to joke papa on his planets. The doctor accepted the jokes in good part, and punished them only with a kiss.

At bottom Mr. Hudelson was not at all a bad fellow, but very obstinate and susceptible withal; so that every one except Loo was chary of treading on his corns. Absorbed in his astronomico-meteorological studies, very jealous of the discoveries he made or claimed to make, he only just managed, in spite of his real affection for Dean Forsyth, to remain the friend of so formidable a rival. They were like two sportsmen shooting over the same preserves. Many were the occasions when Mrs. Hudelson, aided by her two daughters and Francis, intervened to prevent the two astronomers from falling out; and the four peacemakers hoped great things from the marriage. When the two lovers were made one, these threatening storms would be less dangerous. Perhaps the two amateur astronomers might be persuaded to go into partnership, and they might then share the game caught in the celestial hunting-grounds.

Dr. Hudelson's house was a comfortable one. Not one in Whaston was better kept. With a courtyard in front and a garden at the back, where there were fine trees and lawns, it stood in the central portion of Morris Street. Composed of two stories with seven upstairs windows in front, it had to the left of the roof a sort of square tower, thirty yards high, on the top of which was a belvedere. At one of the tower corners rose the mast on which, Sundays and holidays, the Stars and Stripes flag of the United States was hoisted. The top room of the tower was fitted up in view of the special occupations of its owner. There it was that the doctor used his telescopes, save when, on fine nights, he carried them out on to the terrace, whence his gaze could roam freely over the heavens. There it was, too, that, notwithstanding Mrs. Hudelson's recommendations, the doctor caught his worst colds and his sharpest influenzas.

"I'm sure," quoth Miss Loo, "that papa will end by giving the planets his sneezes."

But the doctor would not listen to reason;

and sometimes exposed himself to the severest winter frosts when the thermometer was far below freezing-point, because just then the sky was seen in all its pristine clearness.

From the Morris Street observatory it was easy to perceive the tower of the house in Elizabeth Street. Barely half a mile separated the two dwellings. Between them there was no building and no tree that hindered the view. Without the help of a field-glass it was possible to distinguish the persons standing on either of the towers.

Of course, Dean Forsyth had something else to do than to look at Sydney Hudelson, and Sydney Hudelson was above losing his time in looking at Dean Forsyth. Their observation had a higher pitch. But it was natural that Francis and Jenny should want to find out whether any one were on the opposite terrace, and their eyes often spoke to each other through the medium of their field-glasses. There could be no harm in that.

It would have been feasible to establish telegraphic communication between the two houses. A wire strung from one tower to the other would have facilitated the transmission of agreeable messages between the young people. But their elders, having no need for such sweet discourse, had never thought of such a connection. Perhaps, after the marriage, the thing might be done.

THEIR EYES OFTEN SPOKE TO EACH OTHER THROUGH THE MEDIUM OF THEIR FIELD GLASSES

After the matrimonial bond might come the electric one to join the two families more closely together.

During the afternoon of the same day on which the excellent but shrewish Mitz had given the above-recorded specimen of her eloquence, Francis Gordon called to pay his accustomed visit to Mrs. Hudelson and her daughters—" and her daughter," corrected Loo, pretending to be offended. He was welcomed as if he already belonged to the home. He was not yet Jenny's husband; but Loo insisted on his being her brother; and when Loo insisted on anything, there was no saying her nay.

As for Dr. Hudelson, he was penned up in the tower, and had been since four o'clock in the morning. After appearing late at lunch, just like Dean Forsyth, he had hurried back to his watching, just like Dean Forsyth, exactly at the moment when the sun broke through the clouds. No less preoccupied than his rival, he did not appear disposed to leave his lofty den. And yet it was impossible to decide without him the grand question which was about to be discussed in a general assembly.

" Hallo ! " cried Loo, as the young man entered the drawing-room door, " here is Mr. Francis, the eternal Mr. Francis ! . . . I declare, he's always coming ! "

Francis shook his finger at the incorrigible Loo,

and sat down to go on with a conversation which seemed almost to have continued without interruption from the day before. Indeed, the two lovers, at least in thought, were never separated, which was perhaps why Miss Loo pretended that Francis went out of the front door only to slip in again at the back.

It was the same old subject they talked about, Jenny listening to Francis with a seriousness that took nothing from her charm. They looked at each other and formed plans for the near future. A pretty house had already been found in Lambeth Street, quite suitable for the young couple. It was situated in the West End, not very far from Morris Street, and had a view over the Potomac. Mrs. Hudelson promised to go and examine the place; and, if Jenny approved, it should be taken within the week. Of course, Loo was to accompany her mother and sister. Her opinion was essential.

"By the way," said Loo, "isn't Mr. Forsyth coming to-day?"

"Yes, about four," answered Francis.

"His presence is necessary to settle the matter," observed Mrs. Hudelson.

"Oh! he knows that, and won't fail to keep the appointment," added Francis.

"He had better not," threatened Loo.

"And Mr. Hudelson!" queried Francis. "His presence, too, will be required."

"Father is up in his tower," said Jenny. "He will come down as soon as he is called."

"I will go for him at the proper time," exclaimed Loo. "Six flights of stairs are nothing."

As a matter of fact, both astronomers would have to give their consent to the date fixed for the wedding. Although the principle was accepted of there being no more delay than was unavoidable, the question of bridal attire, especially of that of Miss Loo, complicated things. For the first time in her life Loo was to put on a long dress.

"And if it should not be ready?" joked Francis.

"Then you would have to postpone the wedding," declared Loo, with a laugh that must have mounted up to the observatory.

Right round the clock marched the minute finger, reaching at length the twelve, while the hour finger stood at four. Still Mr. Dean Forsyth did not arrive. In vain Loo leaned out of the window to get a glimpse of the front door. There was no Mr. Forsyth; and there seemed nothing to be done but to be patient. And Loo was not conspicuous for this quality.

"My uncle promised me he would be here to time," said Francis. "But for the last few days he has been quite queer."

"He is not unwell, I hope?" cried Jenny.

"No, but anxious, preoccupied. . . . It's impossible to get him to talk. I can't imagine what is troubling him."

"A splinter from some star or other must have got into his head," suggested Loo.

"My husband is the same," remarked Mrs. Hudelson. "This week he has been more absent-minded than ever. And he sticks up in his den. There must be something extraordinary in the sky."

"I believe you are right," acquiesced Francis. "Uncle refuses to go out; and he hardly sleeps or eats. He forgets even our meal-times."

"Mitz must be in a fine state!" quoth Loo.

"She is in tantrums," replied Francis. "Yet it doesn't make any difference. Uncle used to dread her lectures; but at present he doesn't care for them one bit."

"It's just the same here," said Jenny, smiling. "Loo appears to have lost her influence over father, and you know what that means."

"Is that so, Loo?" asked Francis.

"Yes. But wait a bit. Mitz and I intend to strike a blow that will reduce these naughty folks to submission."

"What can the cause be?" asked Jenny wonderingly.

"Some precious planet they've lost," cried Loo. "I only hope they'll find it again before the wedding."

"We are jesting, and meanwhile Mr. Forsyth doesn't come," interrupted Mrs. Hudelson.

"It will soon be half-past four!" remarked Jenny.

"If my uncle isn't here in five minutes," said Francis, "I will run and fetch him."

At this moment the door-bell rang.

"Mr. Forsyth," pronounced Loo. "Oh! what a racket he makes. I guess he thinks he is listening to a comet fly, and doesn't perceive he's ringing."

The new arrival was indeed Mr. Dean Forsyth. On entering he had to encounter Loo's reproaches.

"Late! late! you deserve a good scolding," was her greeting.

"How do you do, Mrs. Hudelson! how do you do, Jenny dear," said the astronomer, kissing his prospective niece. "Oh, how do *you* do?" he repeated, pinching Loo's cheeks.

All this he said mechanically. As Loo had hinted, his head was filled with something else than his nephew's concerns.

"I was afraid you had forgotten the hour, uncle," said Francis.

"I confess I had, and beg you will excuse me, Mrs. Hudelson," replied the late-comer. "Fortunately, Mitz jogged my memory."

"She was right," said Loo.

"Don't reproach me, my dear," answered Mr. Forsyth, turning to her. "My mind is absorbed just now. I am perhaps on the eve of a most interesting discovery."

"Exactly like papa," began Loo.

"What!" cried the astronomer, springing from the seat on which he had just placed himself. "Do you mean to tell me the doctor . . ."

"Oh! we don't know anything," Mrs. Hudelson hastened to put in, dreading some fresh dispute might arise between her husband and Mr. Forsyth. Then she added, with a view to preventing any further question: "Loo, go and fetch your father."

Light as a bird, the girl flew to the top of the tower; and a minute or so later Mr. Sydney Hudelson arrived in the drawing-room. His face was grave, his eyes were tired, his head so full of blood that he seemed in danger of an apoplectic seizure.

He exchanged greetings with his rival, but their shake-hands was rather a cold one, and each looked the other askance, as if distrust was in their hearts. However, as the two families were gathered for the determining of what Loo punningly called the conjunction of the two planets Francis and Jenny, they had to give their opinion. Since everybody was practically of the same mind, the discussion was a short one. In fact, neither of the two astronomers seemed to notice what was spoken. Their thoughts were elsewhere on the track of the lost asteroid, each asking himself whether the other had discovered it again.

Finally it was agreed that the marriage should take place on the 15th of May, this date allowing time for the furnishing of the bride and bridegroom's new abode.

"And for the finishing of my dress," said Loo demurely.

IV

How two letters sent, one of them to Pittsburg Observatory and the other to Cincinnati Observatory, were docketed and put away in the folio referring to bolides.

To the Head Astronomer of Pittsburg Observatory,
Pennsylvania,

WHASTON, *March the 24th.*

DEAR SIR,

I beg to call your attention to the following fact, which is calculated to be of interest to those studying astronomy. On the morning of the 16th of the present month of March, I discovered a bolide which was passing with considerable velocity through the northern zone of the sky. Its trajectory, somewhere north-south, formed with the meridian an angle of 3° 31′, which I was able to measure accurately. When it appeared in the object-glass of my telescope, the hour was exactly thirty-seven minutes, twenty seconds past seven, and, when it disappeared, thirty-seven minutes, twenty-nine seconds past seven. Since then I have not succeeded in finding it again, notwithstanding the minutest search. I therefore beg you will kindly take note of this information, and acknowledge its receipt, so that, in case of the said meteor becoming visible once more,

I may be guaranteed the title of having been the first to make this valuable discovery.

I remain, dear sir,

Most obediently yours,

Elizabeth Street. DEAN FORSYTH.

To the Head Astronomer of Cincinnati Observatory, Ohio,

WHASTON, *March the 24th.*

DEAR SIR,

On the morning of the 16th of March, between thirty-seven minutes, twenty seconds past seven and thirty-seven minutes, twenty-nine seconds past seven, I was fortunate enough to discover a new bolide which was travelling from north to south in the northern zone of the sky, its apparent direction forming with the meridian a small angle of 3° 31′. Since then I have not succeeded in coming across the trajectory of this meteor. But, if it reappears on our horizon, which I do not doubt, I ought, as a matter of justice, to have the honour of this discovery, which deserves to be recorded in the astronomic annals of our time. I consequently venture to address you this letter, which I should feel much obliged by your acknowledging.

Believe me, Dear Sir,

Most respectfully and faithfully yours,

DOCTOR SYDNEY HUDELSON.

17 Morris Street.

V

In which, in spite of their perseverance, Mr. Dean Forsyth and Dr. Hudelson receive news about their meteor only through the newspapers.

TO the two above letters registered and forwarded, under triple seal, to the head astronomers of Pittsburg and Cincinnati Observatories, the reply would be a simple acknowledgment, and a statement to the effect that they would be duly docketed. The senders asked no more. Both counted on soon having a second view of the bolide. They refused to admit that the asteroid might have rushed far enough away into the depths of the sky to escape the earth's attraction, and that it might never become visible again to the sublunary world. No. Subject to well-determined laws, it would come again within the Whaston horizon. They would be able to perceive it as it passed, to draw attention to it, to calculate its co-ordinates; and it would figure in astronomical charts bearing the glorious name of its discoverer.

But who was the true discoverer? This delicate question would have embarrassed a Solomon even to decide. On the day of the bolide's reappearance there would be two that could claim the title. If Francis Gordon and Jenny Hudelson had known the dangers of the situation, they would certainly have prayed Heaven to see that their marriage was celebrated before this unfortunate meteor reappeared. And the prayer would have been re-echoed by Mrs. Hudelson, Loo, Mitz, and the other friends of the two families.

But nobody did know. With the exception of Dr. Hudelson himself, no inhabitant of Morris Street house troubled about what was occurring in the far-away firmament. In sooth, everybody was busy in other directions. There were visits to pay and receive, as well as compliments; there were invitations to send, presents to be chosen, and many other things to be done too numerous to mention, all of which, as Loo affirmed, made work as arduous as that of Hercules; and there wasn't a moment to lose.

"For the eldest daughter," said Loo, "it is a big affair to get married. One isn't accustomed to it. For the second daughter it's simpler. Everything has been rehearsed. When I get married, you'll see how well I shall manage."

"So, you are thinking of marrying already," observed Francis; "and whom, may I ask?"

"You needn't bother about that," retorted Miss Loo. "It's quite enough for you to know that you are marrying Jenny."

Mrs. Hudelson did as she had promised, and

went to inspect the residence in Lambeth Street. The doctor did not accompany her.

"I leave the matter entirely to you, my dear," he said, "and to Jenny and Francis also, for it concerns them chiefly."

"Will you come down from your tower on the wedding-morning, papa?" asked Loo.

"Of course, my dear, of course."

"And go to Saint Andrew's with Jenny on your arm?"

"Of course, Loo, of course."

"With your black suit and white waistcoat and cravat?"

"Yes, child, yes."

"And will you for once forget your planets, and listen to the sermon that Mr. O'Garth is going to preach so nicely?"

"Why, to be sure, my dear. But we are not yet at the wedding-day; and, since the sky is clear to-day, which is unusual, you can go and inspect the house without me."

Mrs. Hudelson, Jenny, Loo, and Francis, therefore, left the doctor to his telescope, as Mr. Dean Forsyth had been left in Elizabeth Street, and, having gone down Morris Street, they crossed Constitution Square, where they met and saluted the amiable Judge Proth. They then walked up Exeter Street, as Seth Stanfort had done a few days before when waiting for Arcadia Walker, and at last they arrived in Lambeth Street.

THERE, SURROUNDED WITH A BALUSTRADE, THEY FOUND THEMSELVES ON A BIG PLATFORM, WHENCE A SPLENDID VIEW WAS OBTAINED

The house was a pleasant one, well fitted up with the appliances of modern comfort. At the back a study and a dining-room overlooked the garden, which was not very large, but still had some fine, shady trees in it, and was adorned with its first spring flowers. The kitchen and other domestic offices were on the basement floor. The first story was quite equal to the ground-floor, so that Jenny praised her betrothed for having been clever enough to find out so desirable a home. Mrs. Hudelson was equally satisfied with the selection.

This favourable impression was confirmed when the top story of the house was reached. There, surrounded with a balustrade, they found themselves on a big platform whence a splendid view was obtained. Their eyes were able to wander up and down the Potomac, and beyond it to the country town of Steel, which Miss Arcadia had started from to keep her appointment with Seth Stanfort. The whole of Whaston lay spread out before them with its church steeples, high-roofed public buildings, and verdure-crowned trees.

"There's Constitution Square," said Jenny, as she gazed through the field-glass that she had brought with her at Francis' suggestion. "And here's Morris Street. . . . I see our house with the tower and the flag. And there's somebody outside."

"Papa!" pronounced Loo, seizing the field-glass. "I can distinguish him quite plainly. He is manipulating the telescope, but takes good care not to look in our direction. If only we were in the moon!"

"Since you perceive your own house, Loo," interrupted Francis, "you can perhaps make out my uncle's also?"

"Yes," answered Loo. "Wait a bit. It won't be difficult to find the tower. Ah! there the tower is, and there is the house. And I can see somebody up at the top."

"My uncle, no doubt," said Francis.

"He isn't alone."

"Omicron must be with him."

"There is no need to ask what they are doing," remarked Mrs. Hudelson.

"The same as father," said Jenny with a touch of melancholy, she being always a trifle troubled by the two astronomers' rivalry.

When the inspection was finished, and Loo had again expressed her entire approbation, the party returned to the home in Morris Street. On the morrow they would sign the lease, and would begin choosing the furniture, so that everything might be ready for the 15th of May.

In the interval, neither Mr. Dean Forsyth nor Dr. Hudelson intended to waste a single minute, whatever fatigue was caused them by their prolonged watching. So far, in spite of their assiduity, they had not been rewarded by the slightest glimpse of the fugitive.

"Will it ever come back?" sighed Dean Forsyth, after a protracted sojourn in front of his telescope.

"It is bound to come back," answered Omicron, with sublime conviction. "I might even say it is coming back."

"Then why don't we see it?"

"Because it isn't visible."

"How provoking!" again sighed Dean Forsyth. "Any way, if it's invisible to us, it must be invisible to everybody else . . . in Whaston."

"That's certain," assented Omicron.

Thus reasoned master and servitor; and the language they uttered issued from the lips in monologue of Dr. Hudelson also, who was no less discouraged by his want of success.

Both astronomers had received replies to their letters. Pittsburg and Cincinnati Observatories wrote to their respective correspondents, saying that due note had been taken of the information given respecting the passage of a bolide through the northern portion of Whaston horizon on the 16th of March; so far, the observatory telescopes had not succeeded in finding any further trace of the meteor, but, if it should be perceived again, Mr. Dean Forsyth and Dr. Sydney Hudelson would at once be advised of the fact.

Of course each observatory had answered in ignorance that a communication of like import had been made to the other, and that there were consequently two claimants to the honour of being the first discoverer of the bolide.

From the moment these replies were received, the two astronomers might have spared themselves the fatigue of fresh watching. At Pittsburg and Cincinnati there were telescopes much more powerful than their own; and, if the meteor were not a stray body, but had a closed orbit, if, in fine, it were to return under the conditions in which it had first been observed, the two observatories would not fail to detect it. Therefore, Mr. Dean Forsyth and Dr. Sydney Hudelson would have done wisely to trust to the professionals of these two renowned places.

But, as the gentlemen in question were astronomers rather than sages, they went on with their self-imposed task as diligently as ever. Although they had said nothing to each other on the subject, they each suspected the other of being engaged in the same search; and the dread of being anticipated gave them no respite. Jealousy raged in their hearts, and the effect was soon visible in the relations of the two families.

In each home there were anxious hearts. Mr. Dean Forsyth and Dr. Hudelson, once so intimate, forbore to set foot in each other's domicile. Although the two lovers continued to meet every day, it was in a troubled atmosphere. When Francis called at the house in Morris Street, he felt that the doctor was embarrassed by his presence; and, if Mr. Dean Forsyth's name was mentioned, Jenny's father turned pale, then flushed red, whilst his eyes glared and shot an evil look, in spite of his trying to hide it by closing them. Exactly the same symptoms were to be noticed in Francis' uncle. In vain Mrs. Hudelson endeavoured to fathom the cause of this growing coolness and aversion. Her husband merely replied:

"You would not understand. It is useless for me to explain. But I really am astonished at such conduct on the part of Forsyth."

What conduct? Impossible to get him to say. Not even Loo, the spoiled Loo, was able to make her father confess. She wanted to go and question Mr. Forsyth; but Francis dissuaded her. She would only have received a similar statement to the one made by her father. This was proved by Mr. Dean Forsyth's sharp rejoinder to Mitz, who had ventured to interrogate her master.

"Mind your own business," was all the reply she had for her trouble.

Since Francis' uncle dared to speak in this manner to the redoubtable Mitz, the situation must be serious indeed.

As for Mitz, she was flabbergasted—to use her expression. In order to keep herself from cheeking her master back, she stated, she had been obliged to bite her tongue *to the bone*. He was mad, she was quite sure, the madness being caused, according to her, by the inconvenient positions he was forced to assume when gazing into his telescopes, inconvenient especially when certain observations near the zenith obliged him to throw his head back. Mitz concluded that under the strain he had broken something in his *vertical column.*

However, secrets will out. At last Omicron, unable to keep silence any longer, informed the household that his master had discovered an extraordinary bolide, and was afraid Dr. Hudelson should have made the like discovery. So, then, this was the cause of the friends' ridiculous falling out! A meteor! a bolide! an aerolith, a shooting star, a stone, a big stone, granted, but a mere stone after all, against which the nuptial car of Francis and Jenny risked overturning! Loo did not conceal her desire that all meteors might go to Jericho, with the rest of the stars in the firmament!

Meanwhile, the days passed by. March came to an end, and April was now running its course. Soon the wedding-day would arrive. Would no change happen before then? So far, the rivalry was grounded on mere suppositions and hypotheses. What would be the result if some sudden event should bring the two astronomers into open conflict? In spite of these fears, the marriage preparations continued uninterruptedly. Everything would be ready by the date fixed, even Loo's dress.

During the first fortnight of April the weather was abominable: rain, wind, and cloud held undisputed sway. Neither the sun nor the moon, nor, above all, the meteor, was visible. Be it said that Mrs. Hudelson, Jenny, and Francis found no fault with this inclement state of the atmosphere, while Loo for once rejoiced over the persistence of the showers and clouds.

"May they last at any rate till the wedding morning! For the next three weeks I don't want to see the least glimpse of sky," she said.

Loo's prayers were not heard, notwithstanding their fervour. In the night between the 15th and 16th of April, a northern breeze chased away all the vapours, and the heavens showed themselves again in their full brightness. Mr. Dean Forsyth and Dr. Hudelson, perched up in their towers, began once more to scan the Whaston skies from the horizon to the zenith. Now, whatever was the cause or hindrance, and why on the evening of the 17th they neither of them succeeded, any more than they had on the 16th, in detecting any unusual appearance in the object-glass of their telescopes—this must remain unknown. An appearance of something unusual was none the less noticed by others, for in the newspapers of the 19th of April there was the following paragraph:

"The day before yesterday, at nineteen minutes, nine seconds past nine in the evening, a bolide of wonderful size shot through the western atmosphere of the sky at a lightning speed. Singularly enough, this meteor seems to have been, in the first instance, discovered on the same day and at the same hour by two eminent citizens of Whaston, of whom the town is proud. We are informed by the observatory authorities in Pittsburg that this bolide is the same to which their attention was drawn on the 24th of March by Mr. Dean Forsyth; and we are also informed by the observatory authorities in Cincinnati that Dr. Sydney Hudelson wrote to them on this date, giving information of an identical character. We congratulate our two townsmen on their discovery."

VI

Which contains some statements on meteors in general, and on the bolide in particular, which caused the dispute for priority between Mr. Dean Forsyth and Dr. Hudelson.

IF ever a continent might be proud of one of the countries composing it, like a father of one of his children, that continent was North America. If ever a Republic might be proud of one of the States constituting it, that Republic was the United States. If ever one of the States figuring in the stars of the Federal Flag might be proud of its cities, that State was Virginia. And if, in fine, there was a town in Virginia that ought to be proud of its citizens, this town was Whaston, in which such an important addition had just been made to astronomic science.

The foregoing was in fact the opinion of the Whastonians, who felt, as they read the newspaper panegyrics, that the glory of Mr. Dean Forsyth and Dr. Sydney Hudelson was in a manner their own. With the discovery that had been made their town was henceforth indissolubly associated.

Straightway an enthusiastic crowd wended its way to the astronomers' abodes in Morris Street and Elizabeth Street. Of course, none of these admirers had any notion of the rivalry existing between the twin objects of their respect. Both were united in the homage paid. Both names would go down to posterity together, and perhaps even historians in future ages would imagine that the two had been borne by one man. Mr. Dean Forsyth and Dr. Sydney Hudelson, being two separate individuals at present, showed themselves to the crowd, or rather crowds, each on his own balcony, bowing in gratified acknowledgment of the acclamations.

A close observer, however, might have noticed that their attitude did not express an unmixed joy. Their triumph had a shadow that darkened it as a cloud darkens the sun. From one tower to the other sneaked glances of discontent. Each heard the shouts of applause given to his rival, as well as those accorded to himself; and the pleasure of the latter was discounted by the annoyance of the former. In reality, both were cheered with the same heartiness and unanimity. No difference was made between them.

In either house the astronomers and Omicron were the only inhabitants to whom these noisy demonstrations were agreeable. The other members of the two families feared the worst from such an open manifestation of Mr. Dean Forsyth's and the Doctor's equal claims. Mrs. Hudelson and Jenny stood behind the curtains, and con-

In reality, both were cheered with the same heartiness and unanimity

cealed themselves with boding hearts. They saw the likelihood of the two astronomers' making their dispute a public one, and of there being partisans of each, with all the commotion arising from a popular quarrel. And they asked themselves what would be the situation of the bride and bridegroom—a modern Romeo and Juliet—amidst the resuscitated Capulets and Montagues. As for Loo, she was in a rage, and wanted to open the window and speak her mind to these silly people. She regretted even not having a hose and tap at her disposal, so that she might give the crowd a good sprinkle, and drown their hurrahs in torrents of cold water. Her mother and sister had difficulty in restraining her indignation.

Francis' sentiments were almost the same. While his uncle and Omicron were parading above, he was downstairs trying to calm Mitz's anger. Mitz talked of taking her broom and sweeping away the importunate crowd—with the stale. And her threat was not a vain one. There was no doubt that the domestic utensil she used every day so energetically would have been a redoubtable weapon in her hands. Still, it would have seemed scarcely generous to deal so with people that came with good intent.

"Ah! sonny!" she cried to Francis. "Sur-*lie*, those folks must be crazy!"

"I am inclined to believe it," acquiesced Francis.

"All this fuss about a big stone wandering about in the sky."

"Yes, it is foolish!"

"A *meat-door!*"

"A meteor, Mitz," corrected Francis, trying not to laugh.

"What I said, a *meat-door,*" repeated Mitz. "If it could only fall on their heads and smash half a dozen on 'em! Now, I put it to you, you as is a learned man, what's the use of a *meat-door?*"

"To make families fall out," declared Francis, as the hurrahs resounded once more.

Why didn't the two old friends halve their bolide between them? There was no material advantage, no pecuniary profit to be hoped from it. The honour, too, was merely one of name. Why, therefore, grudge there being two names attached to the discovery? Why? Because they were both vain and susceptible. And when these two foibles are in question, what reason is powerful enough to prevail?

After all, what special glory was there in having perceived the meteor? The affair was purely a piece of chance. If the bolide had not been complaisant enough to cross the two astronomers' field of vision just when their eyes were gazing into their telescopes, they would not have discovered it. Every night, hundreds and thousands of such bodies traverse the firmament. It is impossible to count these globes of fire which flash into sight and disappear after a moment. Six hundred millions, such is the number of meteors said by savants to pass through the earth's atmosphere in a single night. These luminous bodies swarm. According to Newton, from ten to fifteen millions can be seen by the naked eye.

"This being so," observed the *Whaston Punch*, the only paper to treat the matter humorously, "it is not so difficult to discover a bolide in the sky as to find a grain of corn in a wheat field; and we venture to think that our two astronomers are beating the big drum rather two loudly over a discovery in which there is little or nothing to discover."

But if the satirical *Punch* thus exercised its comic verve, the serious papers, instead of following suit, seized the opportunity to display their scientific knowledge, which, though very recently acquired, was utilized in such a manner as to render the most authorized professional astronomers jealous.

"Kepler," said the *Whaston Standard*, thought that bolides were produced by terrestrial exhalations. It seems more reasonable to believe that these bodies are simply aeroliths, since they always show traces of violent combustion. In Plutarch's time they were already considered as mineral masses which are flung on to the surface of the earth, when they are caught as they pass, by the terrestrial attraction. The study of bolides proves that their substance is in no wise different from that of minerals known to us, and that, in their totality, they comprise nearly a third of what are termed simple bodies. But how great is the diversity of their elements! These constitutive particles are sometimes as small as iron filings, sometimes as big as peas or nuts, and are remarkably hard, showing in the broken edges traces of crystallization. There are some even which are altogether formed of iron in its primitive state, now and again mixed with nickel, which has never been altered by oxidation."

In sooth, what the *Whaston Standard* told its readers was all very accurate. As a variant, the *Daily Whaston* insisted on the attention paid by ancient and modern savants to these meteoric stones. It said :—

"Diogenes of Apollonia mentions an incandescent stone as large as a mill-stone, whose fall near Ægospotamos terrified the inhabitants of Thrace. If a similar bolide were to fall on Saint Andrew's steeple, it would demolish the tower from summit to base. We may be permitted, in this reference, to mention some of the stones which, coming from the depths of space, and entering into the earth's circle of attraction, fell on to its surface before the Christian era. There was the lightning stone which was adored as the symbol of Cybele in Galatia, and was transported to Rome, as well as another one found in Syria, which was devoted to the worship of the sun. Then, there was the sacred buckler picked up in the reign of Numa; the black stone which is piously kept at Mecca; the thunder-stone which served to fashion the famous sword of Antar. How many aeroliths since the commencement of the Christian era have been described with the circumstances accompanying their fall: a stone of two hundred pounds' weight that fell at Ensisheim in Alsace; a metal-black stone, having the size and shape of a human head, which fell on Mont Vaison in Provence; a stone of fifty-two pounds, having a sulphurous odour, said to be made of meerschaum, which fell at Larini, in Macedonia; a stone that fell at Lucé, near Chartres, in 1763, which was so hot that no one could touch it. Then, there was the bolide which, in 1203, struck the Norman town of Laigle. Humboldt spoke of it as follows: 'At one o'clock in the afternoon, while the sky was quite clear, a large bolide was seen travelling through the air from the south-east to the north-west. A few moments later an explosion was heard, lasting for five or six minutes, which seemed to come from a small black cloud that was almost motionless. This first explosion was followed by three or four detonations and a noise that might have been compared to discharges of musketry with which was mingled the beating of a large number of drums. Each detonation broke from the cloud a portion of the vapours composing it. No luminous appearance was remarked at the spot. More than a thousand meteoric stones fell over an elliptic-shaped surface, the greater axis of which, extending from the south-east to the north-west, measured eleven kilometres in length. These stones smoked and glowed without flame, and were found to be more brittle a few days after their fall than at a subsequent date.'"

The *Daily Whaston* continued in this vein through several columns, and added lavish details, which at least proved the conscientiousness of its editors.

Other papers in the town had also something on the subject. Since astronomy was the question of the day, they became astronomical; and, if, before they finished, there was a single Whastonian left in ignorance of all that concerned bolides, he had only himself to blame.

Vying with the *Daily Whaston*, the *Whaston News* recalled to people's minds the globe of fire, having a diameter double of that of the full moon, which in 1254 was perceived successively at Hurworth, Darlington, Durham, and Dundee, and passed, without bursting, from one horizon to the other, leaving behind it a long luminous trail, golden-coloured, broad, compact, and contrasting sharply with the blue of the sky. The paper added that, if the Hurworth bolide did not burst, such was not the case with the one which, on the 14th of May, was observed at Castillon in France. Although this meteor was visible only for five seconds, its speed was so great that, in this short space of time, it described an arc of six degrees. Its hue, at first, greenish blue, became afterwards white and extraordinarily brilliant. Between the moment when the explosion was perceived and that at which the noise was heard, three or four minutes elapsed, this implying a distance of sixty to eighty kilometres. The violence with which the body burst must, therefore, have been greater than that of the loudest explosions which take place on the surface of the globe. As for the dimensions of this bolide, calculated from its apparent height, its diameter could hardly have been less than fifteen hundred feet; and it must have been travelling at more than a hundred and thirty kilometres per second, a speed infinitely superior to that of the earth in its movement round the sun.

Next, it was the turn of the *Whaston Morning* paper, and then that of the *Whaston Evening*, the latter journal more especially treating of bolides properly so-called, these latter being numerous enough, and having a composition almost entirely ferruginous. It informed its readers that one of these meteoric masses, found in the plains of Siberia, weighed no less than seven hundred kilograms; that another, discovered in Brazil, weighed as much as six thousand kilograms; that a third, fourteen thousand kilograms in weight, had been found at Olympus in Tucuman; that a fourth, which fell in the environs of Duranzo, in Mexico, had the enormous weight of nineteen thousand kilograms.

To tell the truth, some of the Whastonian population were alarmed on reading these articles. Since the meteor discovered by Messrs. Forsyth and Hudelson had been perceived under the conditions and at the distance already related, it must have dimensions superior probably to those of the Tucuman and Duranzo bolides. Perhaps its size might equal or even exceed that of the Castillon aerolith with the fifteen hundred foot diameter. Now, if the said meteor had appeared in the zenith of Whaston, the town of Whaston must be situated in its trajectory. And, if the trajectory had an orbit, the bolide would again pass over the town. Suppose that the bolide should, through some cause or other, stop in its course just at this time, Whaston would be struck, with results that could scarcely be conceived. Now or never, it was the moment to teach the inhabitants, if they were ignorant, the terrible law of living force, and, if they knew it, to refresh their memory: *the mass multiplied by the square of the velocity*—a velocity which, in accordance with the still more terrifying law of falling bodies, and for a bolide falling from a height of four hundred kilometres, would attain nearly three thousand metres a second at the moment when the mass crashed down on the surface of the earth.

The Whastonian press did not fail in its duty; and in justice it must be stated that never had daily newspapers indulged before in such a display of mathematical formulæ. Gradually the town was worked up to a pitch of excitement. The dangerous bolide became the subject of all conversations on the public Square, in social reunions as in family circles. The feminine portion of the population, in particular, could think of nothing but smashed churches and annihilated houses. As for the men, they deemed it more becoming to shrug their shoulders, but the shrugs were very perfunctory. Night and day, we might almost say, on Constitution Square, as in the higher quarters of the town, groups were to be seen standing. Whether the sky was clear or cloudy, there were observers watching. Never had opticians sold so many field-glasses, spectacles, and other instruments for aiding sight! Never had the heavens been gazed at so much as by the anxious eyes of the Whastonians! Whether the meteor were visible or not, the danger was present, at every hour, not to say every minute, and every second.

It threatened even the neighbourhood, the towns, hamlets, and villages situated beneath the trajectory. Yet Whaston was the place where the fear was greatest, for the simple reason that at Whaston the bolide had been first perceived.

There was one paper, however, which continued to the last to make light of these fears—the paper which, we have already said, had joked the two astronomers on their discovery, and which now, still jesting, rendered them responsible for the disasters that menaced the town. What business was it of these gentlemen, said *Punch*, to go tickling space with their telescopes? Couldn't they leave the firmament alone and forbear teasing the stars? Were there not real savants enough who meddled with what did not concern them, and indiscreetly insinuated themselves among the intrastellar zones? "The celestial bodies are shy," said *Punch*, "and do not like to be looked at close to. Yes, our city is in peril; no one is safe at present, and there is no remedy possible. Against fire, hail, and cyclones there is insurance; but how can you insure against the fall of a bolide perhaps ten times as large as the citadel of Whaston? . . . And if it should burst and scatter when falling, which frequently happens with things of this kind, the whole town will be bombarded, and fired too, if the projectiles are incandescent! In any case, the destruction of our dear city is inevitable; there is no disguising the matter! Let each person look to himself, and the devil take the hindmost! Zounds! why didn't Messrs. Forsyth and Hudelson stay quietly in the lower stories of their dwellings, instead of spying on meteors? They are the guilty ones, who have drawn down this vengeance. If Whaston is destroyed by this bolide, the fault will be theirs! . . . We ask every reader of the *Whaston Punch,* that is to say every impartial reader, to tell us what is the utility of astronomers, astrologers, meteorologists, and other ologists. What good has ever resulted from their labours? . . . To ask the question is to answer it. And, as for ourselves, we agree with the opinion so well expressed by the Frenchman, Brillat-Savarin: 'The discovery of a new dish does more for human happiness than the discovery of a star?' Small indeed would have been the esteem of Brillat-Savarin for these two maleficent astronomers who have not hesitated to involve their country in the worst of all catastrophes simply for the pleasure of spying out a bolide."

VII

In which Mrs. Hudelson appears much annoyed at the Doctor's attitude, and Mitz is heard to snub her master.

WHAT did Mr. Dean Forsyth and Dr. Hudelson reply to these pleasantries of the *Whaston Punch?* Nothing, seeing that they remained in ignorance of what this disrespectful paper had published about them. To be ignorant of the disagreeable things that are said about us is the surest way not to suffer from them. But, if the two astronomers knew nothing of the satire, their families and friends were less fortunate; and Mitz was particularly affected. It was a crime to accuse her master of being responsible for this danger that threatened the town! . . . Mr. Forsyth ought to prosecute the author of the article; and Judge Proth would be sure to give heavy damages to the plaintiff, and perhaps imprisonment to the libeller.

Little Loo, also, took the thing seriously; but she approved the *Whaston Punch.* Without Mr. Forsyth and her papa, the confounded meteor would have gone by and done no damage. The damage she was thinking of was the disturbance of the relations between the two families in Morris Street and Elizabeth Street. What Loo dreaded came to pass.

No sooner had the newspapers published the reports of the Pittsburg and Cincinnati observatories, and it was officially announced that they both had a right to the discovery of the bolide, than each of them ceased to make the slightest allusion to the wedding. If any one else spoke of it, they immediately invented a pretext for withdrawing to their towers, where, indeed, they spent nearly all their time, more absorbed and preoccupied than ever.

Not that their perseverance was rewarded. Whether it were that the meteor was now at a distance too great for their telescopes to see it, or whether there were some other hindrance, they wore themselves out in their efforts to calculate the elements of the asteroid, of which they persisted in deeming themselves respectively the sole and exclusive discoverer. There was one way only of settling the dispute between them; and this way was to prove which of the two was the better mathematician. To him would be awarded the palm.

But their unique observation had been too short for a proper basis to be afforded for their formulæ. Another observation, perhaps several, would be necessary before the orbit of the bolide could be determined with any certainty. This was why Mr. Dean Forsyth and Dr. Hudelson, each fearing to be outdone by his rival, watched the heavens with like but useless zeal. The capricious meteor made no further appearance over the Whaston horizon, or, if it reappeared, did so in the strictest incognito.

The temper of both astronomers grew worse in proportion to the continued failure attending their vigils. Every one dreaded to go near them. Twenty times a day Mr. Forsyth waxed angry with Omicron, who answered him with a sharpness of tone equal to his own. The Doctor, having no assistant, was compelled to give vent to his wrath without hearers—except himself. And himself had to listen to some singular language.

Three days had sped since the publication of the notes sent to the newspapers from the observatories. The celestial clock, the hand of which is the sun, would have struck the 22nd of April, if the Chief Clockmaker had bethought himself to supply an apparatus for striking. Another twenty days, and the great date would arrive, although Loo—in her impatience—asserted that it did not exist in the calendar.

After discussion, Mrs. Hudelson decided that the best plan would be to say nothing at all to her husband until the wedding morning, and then to say simply:

"Here are your hat and coat and gloves. It is time to go to St. Andrew's. Let us start."

He would go undoubtedly, without troubling

to ask why, unless the meteor should happen to pass at the same moment in front of his telescope.

In his house in Elizabeth Street, Mr. Dean Forsyth did not get off so easily, Mitz having a temper as well as her master, and being more and more indignant over his attitude towards the marriage of "sonny," resolved to give the astronomer a piece of her mind. Consequently, in the afternoon of the 22nd of April, happening to be alone with Mr. Dean Forsyth in the dining-room, she stopped him just as he was making for the staircase leading to the tower. Already only too familiar with Mitz's tongue, the astronomer saw by a glance at her face, which was like a bomb with a burning match attached to it, threatening to explode, what he had to expect, and he continued his retreat. But, ere he could open the door, the old servant, thrusting herself in his path, said:

"Sir, I have a few words to speak to you."

"To speak to me, Mitz?" replied the astronomer timidly. "Just now I am in a hurry."

"Sakes! sir, me too, seeing I've got all the plates and dishes to wash. Your *tubes* can wait as well as my dishes."

"But Omicron is calling me, I think."

"*My Crown?* . . . He's a *nice cup o' tea,* he is! He'll hear from me one of these fine mornings, will *My Crown.* You can tell him I said so. A wink's as good as a nod to a blind horse."

"I will, Mitz. But my bolide?"

"Your *bow-lid!*" repeated Mitz. "I don't know what that is. All my eye and Betty Martin, I dare say."

"A bolide, Mitz," explained Mr. Dean Forsyth patiently, "is a meteor, and . . ."

"Ah!" cried Mitz, "so it's the famous *meat door!* . . . Well, let it wait, like *My Crown*, let it wait."

"On my word!" exclaimed Mr. Forsyth, his susceptibility being aroused.

"And," continued Mitz, "as the sky is overcast, and it's going to rain, it ain't any use amusing yourself with looking up at nothing."

Truly, in the persistence of this bad weather, both Mr. Dean Forsyth and Dr. Hudelson had something to upset their equanimity. For a couple of days now, the sky had been again covered with thick clouds. During the day not a bit of sun; and during the night not a star to be seen. White vapours twisted and twirled from one horizon to the other, like a veil that the spire of Saint Andrew's sometimes pierced with its summit. Under these circumstances, it was impossible to make any observations, and to see the bolide. Indeed, the various official observatories must be just as unsuccessful, if, as was probable, they had to contend with the same unfavourable conditions. And, as a matter of fact, no fresh information concerning the appearance of the meteor had

"WELL, LET IT WAIT"

been inserted in the newspapers. Be it granted that this meteor was not of such interest that the scientific world was likely to take much notice of it. The phenomenon was a very commonplace one; and no one but a Dean Forsyth or a Hudelson would have watched for its return with an impatience of this frenzied character.

As soon as Mitz was sure that her master could not escape, she crossed her arms, and went on with her lecture:

"Mr. Forsyth, have you forgotten that you have a nephew named Francis Gordon?"

"No!" replied the astronomer, with debonair mien. "I have not forgotten. Of course not! And how is the dear fellow getting on?"

"Very well, sir, thank you."

"I've not seen him, I think, for some little time."

"That's so, sir, not since lunch."

"Really!"

"Are you always star-gazing, sir?" asked Mitz, forcing her master to turn round to her.

"No, certainly not, Mitz! . . . But, I admit, I am a little bit taken up at present."

"Taken up, to the point of forgetting something that's important."

"Forgetting something that's important? . . . What's that?"

"Your nephew is going to get married."

"Get married! . . . Get married! . . ."

"You're not going to ask me who the lady is, I hope?"

"No, Mitz! . . . But why are you asking me these questions?"

"Oh! that's all very fine. A question means an answer."

"An answer what about, Mitz?"

"About your conduct, sir—your behaviour to the Hudelsons! . . . I suppose you know there's a family named Hudelson. a Dr. Hudelson, who lives in Morris Street, a Mrs. Hudelson, the mother of Miss Loo Hudelson, and Miss Jenny Hudelson, who is to marry your nephew?"

Mitz brought out the name Hudelson each time with increased emphasis, and Mr. Dean Forsyth put his hand to his chest, to his side, to his head, as if the word were a bullet that had been fired at him at close quarters. He suffered, he choked, the blood rushed to his brain. Seeing that he did not reply, Mitz said:

"Well! did you hear me?"

"Of course I heard you!" cried her master.

"Well?" repeated the old servant in a louder tone.

"Is Francis still intending to go on with this marriage?" asked Mr. Forsyth finally.

"I should think he is, the same as we all are, and you, too, I hope?"

"What! my nephew is resolved to marry this Dr. Hudelson's daughter?"

"Miss Jenny, if you please, sir. You may bet your bottom dollar he is, sir. He'd be off his chump if he wasn't. Where 'ud he find anybody nicer?"

"Even admitting," interrupted Mr. Forsyth, "that the daughter of the man who . . . the man who . . . the man whose name I cannot pronounce without its sticking in my throat, is a nice girl . . ."

"I can't bear it!" cried Mitz, undoing her apron, as if she were going to throw it down.

"Come . . . Mitz . . . come," murmured her master, a trifle disturbed by so threatening an attitude.

The old servant brandished her apron with its strings hanging down to the floor.

"I've had enough," she said. "After fifty years' service, I'd sooner go and die in a corner like a mangy dog than stay with a man that wrongs his own flesh and blood. I'm only a poor servant, but I've got a heart, sir, if you haven't."

"But, Mitz," answered the astronomer, vexed; "don't you know what this Hudelson has done to me?"

"What's he done?"

"He has robbed me."

"Robbed you!"

"Yes, robbed me abominably."

"Has he stolen your watch . . . your purse . . . your handkerchief!"

"No . . . my bolide!"

"Ah! your *bow-lid!*" laughed the old servant sarcastically. "Your famous *meat-door!* Sakes! is it possible to get into such tantrums over a gadabout *meat-door!* Is it yours any more than it is the doctor's? Have you put your name on it? Don't it belong to everybody, to anybody, to me, to my dog, if I had one . . . but I haven't, thank goodness! . . . Have you bought it out of your own pocket, or have you had it left you . . ."

"Mitz! . . ." cried Mr. Forsyth, now in a passion.

"Don't Mitz me!" said the old servant, fairly boiling over. "You're as *stoopid as old Saturn* (she probably meant Satan) to fall out with a friend about a dirty stone that you'll neither of you see again."

"Hold your tongue! hold your tongue!" protested the astronomer, who was stung to the quick.

"No, sir, I shan't hold my tongue; and, if you like, you can call to your silly *My Crown* to help you."

"Silly Omicron!"

"Yes, silly, and he won't make me hold my tongue either . . . any more than our President himself couldn't silence the archangel Michael, coming to say it's the end of the world."

Mr. Dean Forsyth was dumbfounded on hearing this terrible sentence. His throat contracted, and no words would issue from it. Had he wished to dismiss the faithful but shrewish Mitz from his service, he would have been unable to pronounce the sentence of dismissal.

Not that Mitz would have gone, even if he had found his voice. After half a century she didn't intend to quit the master she had known from his birth, on account of an unlucky meteor. It was time, however, this scene should finish; and the astronomer being aware that he was beaten, sought some means of escape that might not seem too undignified.

Happily the sun lent him its aid, appearing through the window that overlooked the garden. As soon as he saw it, he instantly thought of Dr. Hudelson up in his belvedere, and saw his rival profiting by this opportunity to sweep the heavens with his telescope. The sun's rays produced the same effect on him as on a balloon filled with gas. It swelled him, gave him ascensional power, and obliged him to rise in the atmosphere. Mr. Dean Forsyth, casting from him (this, to complete the metaphor) the ballast of all his anger, approached the door once more.

Unfortunately, Mitz blocked the way, and did not seem disposed to let him pass. It looked as though he would be obliged to use force, and to summon Omicron to help him. However, just at this moment, the old servant, who was exhausted by the scene, and was also agitated by her fears for her sonny, sank down on a chair, altogether overcome. The astronomer, be it said to his credit, momentarily forgot the sun, the blue sky, and the meteor. Going to Mitz, he asked her what she was suffering from.

"I don't know, sir; my stomach is all upside down," she faltered.

"Stomach upside down?" repeated her master, bewildered by the mention of this singular malady.

"Yes, sir," said Mitz, with dolent voice; "my heart is shaking me to bits."

"Hum!" pronounced Mr. Dean Forsyth, whose perplexity was not diminished by this second statement.

However, he thought he must do something, and was about to proceed to loosen the patient's stays, and to rub her temples with vinegar. But, before he had time to carry out his intentions, Omicron's voice resounded from the summit of the tower.

"The bolide, sir! the bolide!" cried his assistant.

The astronomer lost sight of the rest of the universe on the instant, and bounded into the staircase. No sooner had he disappeared than Mitz recovered the use of her limbs and faculties, and rushed to the foot of the stairs up which her master was flying three steps at a time. In loud tones, she shouted up the spiral:

"Just remember, Mr. Forsyth, sir, that Francis' marriage with Jenny Hudelson will take place, and at the time fixed. It will take place, sir, or *I'll be non-plussed.*"

The astronomer did not answer; in fact, he did not hear what was said. He was already at the top of the tower.

VIII

In which press polemics aggravate the situation, which ends in a discovery as incontestable as it is unexpected.

"IT'S the same, Omicron; it's the same!" cried Mr. Dean Forsyth, as soon as he put his eye to the telescope.

"The same!" echoed Omicron. "Let's hope Dr. Hudelson isn't on the top of his observatory just now."

"Or if he is," said his master, "let's hope he can't see the bolide."

"Our bolide," added Omicron.

"My bolide," unconsciously corrected his master.

Both were mistaken. At this very moment Dr. Hudelson's telescope was directed towards the south-east, which was the part of the sky then being traversed by the meteor. And no less than his rival, the doctor kept his eyes fixed on the phenomenon until it vanished in the mists of the south. Indeed, the two Whaston astronomers were not the only observers of the bolide on this occasion. It was perceived by the Pittsburg Observatory likewise.

This return of the meteor was an occurrence of the highest interest—if it can be asserted that the meteor itself had any interest. Since it remained in view of the sublunary world, it was evidently travelling in a closed orbit, and was not one of those shooting stars which, after striking the upper strata of the air, finally disappear, or one of those aeroliths which fall to earth almost as soon as they are noticed. No, it was a recurrent meteor, revolving round the globe, like a second satellite. It therefore merited attention, and furnished some excuse for the eagerness displayed by Mr. Dean Forsyth and Dr. Hudelson, and for their endeavours to appropriate it.

Since the meteor obeyed constant laws, there was nothing to hinder its elements being calculated. The attempt was made in various quarters; but, as may be supposed, nowhere with more activity than at Whaston. Yet, in order that the problem might be entirely solved, a number of further favourable observations would be required.

The first result obtained, a couple of days later, by mathematicians who were not Dean Forsyth or Sydney Hudelson, was the bolide's trajectory, which lay in an exact north-south direction. The slight deviation of 3°, 31′ mentioned by Mr. Dean Forsyth in his letter to the Pittsburg Observatory was only an apparent one, and was caused by the rotation of the terrestrial globe.

Four hundred kilometres separated the bolide from the earth's surface, and its prodigious velocity was not less than six thousand nine hundred and sixty-seven metres per second. It therefore accomplished its journey round the globe in one hour, forty-one minutes, forty-one seconds, ninety-three-hundredths of a second; whence the conclusion that it would not appear again under the zenith of Whaston before the lapse of a hundred and four years, seventy-six days, twenty-two hours. This last statement was calculated to reassure the town's inhabitants, who were so much dreading the fall of the troublesome asteroid. If it fell, they would not be the victims.

"But what reason is there for thinking it will fall?" asked the *Whaston Morning* paper. "There is no likelihood of its meeting with any obstacle on its way, or of its being otherwise checked in its movement."

This was plain.

"We grant," said the *Whaston Evening* paper, "that some of these aeroliths have fallen, and do fall still. But they are generally small, wander about in space, and fall only when the earth's attraction is too strong for them."

Certainly the bolide in question was not of this sort. Travelling in a regular orbit, its fall was no more to be feared than that of the moon. This point being established, there were several others to be elucidated before any one could claim to be well informed concerning the asteroid which, so to speak, had become a second satellite of the earth.

What was its volume? What was its mass? What its nature? To the first question, the *Whaston Standard* replied as follows:

"Judging by the bolide's apparent height and dimensions, its diameter must be over five hundred metres, at any rate, this is what the observations so far made seem to indicate. But its nature no one has yet been able to determine. Seen through instruments sufficiently powerful, it shines with great brilliancy, this latter being no doubt due to atmospheric friction, although, at such an altitude, the density of the air is not great. Possibly the meteor is nothing more than a mass of gaseous composition. Or, on the other hand, it may be composed of a solid nucleus with a luminous coma. In the second case, what is the size and nature of the nucleus? Probably, we shall never know.

"In fine, this bolide is not an extraordinary one, either by its volume or by its velocity. Its only peculiarity is that it revolves in a closed orbit. For how long has it so revolved round our globe? The most skilled astronomers of our observatory would not be able to tell us, since they would never have perceived it through their official telescopes but for our two fellow-townsmen, Mr. Dean Forsyth and Dr. Sydney Hudelson, to whom the glory of this magnificent discovery has been reserved."

The scientific world, being of the *Whaston*

Standard's opinion that the bolide was not an extraordinary one, did not trouble to notice the innuendo placed at the close of this writer's article. And the unscientific world outside Whaston manifested pretty much the same indifference. Perhaps even the citizens of Whaston would have soon grown tired of what *Punch* termed a comic incident, if certain newspapers had not begun to hint more and more plainly at the dispute which was simmering between Mr. Dean Forsyth and Dr. Hudelson. No sooner was this fact made public than rumour laid hold of it. The dispute was made a public matter, and the town began to split into two opposite camps.

Meanwhile the date of the marriage drew near. Mrs. Hudelson, Jenny, and Loo, on the one hand, and Francis Gordon and Mitz, on the other, lived in a state of anxiety that increased rather than diminished. They were in constant fear that a meeting between the two rivals might provoke some outbreak, just as the shock of two clouds charged with contrary electricities produces thunder and lightning. It was known that Mr. Dean Forsyth's anger still persisted, and that Mr. Hudelson's wrath needed only an occasion to manifest itself.

The sky remained on the whole fine at present; the atmosphere was pure; the Whaston horizons were clear; so that the two astronomers were able to multiply their observations. And their opportunities were numerous, since the bolide reappeared above the horizon more than fourteen times in the twenty-four hours, and they now knew, thanks to the data supplied by the State observatories, the precise point towards which at each passage of the meteor their telescopes must be directed.

Of course, the convenience of these observations varied with the height of the bolide above the horizon. But the latter's appearances were so frequent that a little inconvenience occasionally did not matter. If the bolide returned no longer under the mathematic zenith of Whaston, where, by a miraculous chance, it had been perceived in the first instance, it came so close to this position each day that the difference was a negligible quantity.

Indeed, the two astronomers could regale themselves with the contemplation of this meteor ploughing through the sky above their heads, and splendidly adorned with a brightly shining aureole! They feasted their eyes on it. Each of them called it by his own name, the Forsyth bolide, the Hudelson bolide. It was their child, flesh of their flesh. It belonged to them as the son to his parents, or, better still, as the creature to its creator. The sight of it excited them without ceasing. Their observations, the hypotheses they formed respecting its movements, its apparent form, they addressed to the Cincinnati

Observatory, the one, and to the Pittsburg Observatory, the other, not forgetting, of course, to claim priority for what had been observed each time.

But now this specific competition no longer satisfied their inimical feelings. Not content with having broken off diplomatic relations, they wanted open hostilities, with an official declaration of war. There appeared, one day, in the *Whaston Standard*, a somewhat aggressive paragraph against the doctor, which was attributed to Mr. Dean Forsyth. The paragraph said that some people's eyes were good only when they looked through other people's glasses, and that they saw only what had been already seen. To this a paragraph in the *Whaston Evening* replied that object-glasses were sometimes badly wiped, and that spots were left on them which it was easy to mistake for meteors. At the same time, *Punch* published a caricature with striking likenesses of the two rivals, who were represented with gigantic wings, flying to catch the bolide, the latter having a zebra's head with its tongue thrust out fleeringly.

Although, in consequence of these annoying allusions, the quarrel of the two astronomers grew more bitter every day, neither the one nor the other of them had so far had an opportunity of interfering with the marriage preparations. If they said nothing, at least they did nothing either ; so that the supposition still was that on the day appointed Francis and Jenny would be united together with the golden knot. The last days of April ran their course. At Mr. Hudelson's the meals passed off with hardly a word at table. By her mother's order, Loo refrained from mentioning the meteor, but, by the way she cut her meat, it was evident she was wishing she could have crushed the bolide out of existence as easily. Jenny's sadness was visible enough for the doctor to have noticed it, had he not been so preoccupied with his own reflections.

Naturally, Francis did not appear at meal-times. His daily visit was paid only when Mr. Hudelson was safe up in his tower. And at his own home meals were not very cheerful either. Mr. Dean Forsyth scarcely ever spoke, and Mitz, when addressed by her master, answered with a short "yes" or "no."

On the 28th of April, however, on rising from lunch, Francis' uncle said to him:

"Do you still go to the Hudelsons'?"

"Certainly, uncle," replied Francis, with a firm voice.

"Why shouldn't he go to the Hudelsons'?" asked Mitz in a tone of anger.

"I didn't speak to you, Mitz," muttered Mr. Forsyth.

"Well, I am speaking to you, sir," Mitz retorted. "A cat may look and *mew* at a king."

Mr. Forsyth shrugged his shoulders and turned to Francis.

"I go there every day," added the latter.

"After what the doctor has done to me?"

"What has he done to you?"

"He has allowed himself to discover . . ."

"What you discovered yourself," interrupted Francis; "what everybody had the right to discover . . . a bolide. There are plenty of them in sight of Whaston."

"You are wasting your breath, sonny," sneered Mitz. "Don't you see your uncle is quite gone on his stone, which, after all, is about as 'straordinary as the mile-stone outside our house."

Thus expressed herself Mitz; and Mr. Dean Forsyth, exasperated by such language, said wrathfully:

"Anyway, Francis, I forbid you to set foot again inside the doctor's door."

"I regret to disobey you, uncle," answered Francis, making an effort to keep his temper; "but I shall go."

"Yes, he will go," cried Mitz, "even if you were to chop him into pieces."

"Then you persist in your plans?" queried the astronomer, disdaining to notice Mitz's remark.

"Yes, uncle."

"And you intend to marry the daughter of this thief?"

"Yes; nothing will prevent me."

"We shall see."

And with these words, the first that indicated his resolution to oppose the marriage, Mr. Dean Forsyth quitted the room and mounted the staircase leading to the tower, slamming the door after him.

As Francis walked to Morris Street that afternoon, he asked himself whether he might not have to meet with a similar prohibition from the doctor. To neither Mrs. Hudelson nor to her daughters did he mention what his uncle had said, and endeavoured to hide his anxiety. It was of no use to increase the trouble they themselves had to bear. Reasoning with himself, he found it difficult, indeed, to believe that any real obstacle could arise to his marriage from this bolide. Even supposing the doctor and his uncle declined to come to the wedding, it could take place without them, unless Jenny's father should hinder Mr. O'Garth from performing the ceremony.

As if to encourage him in his optimism, some days went by without any further incident. The weather continued fine, and the sky as clear as Whaston had ever enjoyed it. With the exception of a few morning and evening mists that melted away after the rising and setting of the sun, nothing troubled the purity of the atmosphere, in which the bolide accomplished its regular revolution. The two astronomers revelled in the sight; while Mitz, on the contrary, shook her fist at the sky each night as she went to bed.

Alas! her threat was vain. Still the meteor circled in the starry welkin.

And still, also, the public intervened in the quarrel more and more markedly. Sides were taken by the newspapers, violently in some cases, with the two rival claimants. None remained quite indifferent. It was announced that meetings would be held to discuss the merits of the case. And with what intemperance of language may be imagined! Francis and his betrothed were at their wits' end to know what to do, especially as in the papers conversations were related that were attributed to Dr. Hudelson and Mr. Dean Forsyth, and the words uttered, or said to have been uttered, became less and less polite.

When things had reached this point something occurred that made the affair not merely now of American, but of world-wide notoriety. It was not the explosion of the bolide, but a piece of news that the telegraph and telephone flashed throughout all the kingdoms and republics of the old and new hemispheres. The said information came neither from Mr. Hudelson's tower, nor from that of Mr. Dean Forsyth. It did not come from the Boston Observatory, nor yet from that of Cincinnati. This time it was the Paris Observatory which produced a commotion all over the globe. A paragraph was inserted in the French press as follows:

" The bolide, to which the attention of the Cincinnati and Pittsburg Observatories was drawn by two honourable citizens of the town of Whaston, State of Virginia, and which appears to be accomplishing its revolution round the earth with perfect regularity, is being studied at present night and day in all the observatories in the world by a body of eminent astronomers, whose thorough competence is only equalled by their admirable devotion to the cause of science.

"If, in spite of this careful examination, several parts of the problem are still unsolved, the Paris Observatory has, at any rate, succeeded in solving one, having determined the nature of this meteor.

"The rays emanating from the bolide have been submitted to spectrum analysis, and the arrangement of their lines has allowed the substance of the luminous body to be recognized with certainty.

"Its nucleus, which is surrounded with a brilliant coma, and from which the rays issue, is not of a gaseous nature, but solid. It is not ferruginous, like many aeroliths, nor is it formed of any chemical compounds that usually make up these wandering bodies.

"This bolide is in gold, pure gold, and, if its real value cannot be indicated, the reason is that so far success has not attended the efforts made to measure the dimensions of its nucleus exactly."

Such was the information conveyed to the whole world. It is more difficult to describe the effect produced than to conjure up this effect in the imagination. A globe of gold, a mass of precious metal, the value of which must be several milliards, was revolving round the earth! What dreams this sensational news aroused! What desires it awoke in every country, and more especially in the town of Whaston, which had the honour of its discovery, and, most of all, in the hearts of the town's two citizens, henceforward immortal—Dean Forsyth and Sydney Hudelson!

IX

In which the newspapers, the public, Mr. Dean Forsyth, and Dr. Hudelson go in for mathematics.

IN gold! It was in gold! The first sentiment was incredulity. Some people thought the thing was a mistake which would soon be rectified; others that it was a huge hoax concocted by jokers of the first water. If so, no doubt the Paris Observatory would at once contradict the statement.

But no disclaimer came. On the contrary, the astronomers of all countries, having repeated the experiments of their French *confrères*, confirmed the conclusions arrived at, *nemine contradicente*. Consequently, every one was obliged to accept the strange phenomenon with its explanation. The excitement was enormous.

When an eclipse of the sun occurs, the sale of optical instruments augments in considerable proportions. It was the same now. People rushed to buy whatever lay within their means for the purpose of getting a nearer glimpse of the bolide, which was gazed at and admired more than sovereign, or actress, or ballerine by the enthusiastic public, while it pursued its onward, regular career in the infinity of space.

The fine weather continued, so that Mr. Dean Forsyth and Dr. Hudelson were practically fixtures in their respective towers, both of them seeking to add to the information already possessed concerning the nature of the mysterious meteor. If the question of priority in the discovery could not be settled satisfactorily, they meant at least to struggle for the honour of learning most about their property.

In all parts of the world the bolide had become the one thing of interest. Unlike the Gauls, whose only fear was that the sky might fall on their heads, humanity at present unanimously desired that the bolide would stop in its course, and, yielding to the earth's attraction, fall and enrich the globe with its wandering milliards.

What calculations were made to establish the number of these milliards! Unfortunately, these calculations lacked any reliable basis, since the dimensions of the nucleus remained unknown. The value of the nucleus, whatever it was, could not, indeed, fail to be prodigious; and this was enough to inflame every one's imagination.

On the 3rd of May the *Whaston Standard* published an article which terminated as follows:

"Admitting that the nucleus of the Forsyth-Hudelson bolide is constituted by a sphere measuring only ten metres in diameter, this sphere would, if in iron, weigh three thousand, seven hundred

GAZED AT AND ADMIRED . . . BY THE ENTHUSIASTIC PUBLIC

and sixty-three tons. But the same sphere, formed of pure gold, would weigh ten thousand and eighty-three tons, and would be worth nearly six thousand millions of dollars."

"Is it possible, sir?" asked Omicron, after reading the article just quoted.

"It is certain," replied Mr. Dean Forsyth. "To be convinced, you have only to multiply the mass by the mean value of gold, that is to say, five hundred and seventy-four dollars per kilogram, the mass being the product of the density of the metal multiplied by the volume, that is to say, 19.258. As for the volume, it is obtained by the formula: $V=\frac{\pi D^3}{6}$.

"Ah! yes! . . ." approved Omicron, as though he understood.

"The annoying feature of the article," added Mr. Dean Forsyth, "is its persisting in coupling my name with that of this individual!"

Probably Dr. Hudelson made the same reflection to himself. Miss Loo, who happened also to have scanned the article in question, curled her lips with sufficient disdain for the millions of dollars to have been humiliated, could they have been conscious of it.

The temperament of journalists leading them generally to go one better always, the *Whaston Evening* replied to the *Standard* in terms that evinced marked partiality to the Morris Street astronomer. It said:

"We cannot understand why the *Standard* should have been so modest in its calculations. We are inclined to be bolder. Without venturing outside hypotheses that are reasonable, we will attribute a diameter of a hundred metres to the nucleus of Hudelson's bolide. Taking this figure as a basis, we find that the weight of such a sphere of gold would be ten millions, ninety-three thousand, four hundred and eighty-eight tons, and that its value would be not far short of six billions of dollars."

"It is just as well to neglect the cents," commented *Punch*.

These possibilities stimulated the two Whaston astronomers to greater activity in their researches, if such could be. Each, favoured by the barometer at "set fair," strove to establish the dimensions of the asteroid's nucleus. This, however, was not easy, on account of the brilliant coma. Once, during the night between the 5th and 6th, Mr. Dean Forsyth thought he had success within his fingers. The irradiation having for a moment diminished, a glittering globe showed itself distinctly.

"Omicron," shouted Mr. Dean Forsyth, his voice rendered hollow through emotion.

"Sir?"

"The nucleus!"

"Yes . . . I see it."

"At last! we've got it!"

"Oh!" cried Omicron, "it's hidden again."

"YES . . . I SEE IT"

"Never mind! I've seen it! . . . I shall have had this glory! To-morrow, the first thing, we'll telegraph to the Pittsburg Observatory; . . . and that wretch, Hudelson, won't be able this time to pretend . . ."

Was Mr. Dean Forsyth under a delusion, or had Dr. Hudelson on this single occasion allowed his rival to gain an advantage over him? We shall never know; and, what is more, the intended telegram was not sent to the Pittsburg Observatory, for this reason, that, in all the next morning's papers throughout the world, the following information appeared:

"The Greenwich Observatory has the honour to apprise the public that, from calculations made at the observatory, and a series of observations of most satisfactory character, the bolide first seen by two honourable citizens of Whaston and recognized by the Paris Observatory to be composed of pure gold, is constituted by a sphere of a hundred and ten metres' diameter, and has a volume of about six hundred and ninety-six thousand cubic metres.

"Such a sphere, in gold, ought to weigh more than thirteen million tons. Calculations prove that this is not the case. The real weight of the bolide is scarcely a seventh of the just mentioned figures, and is something like one million, eight hundred and sixty-seven thousand tons, a weight corresponding to a volume of about ninety-seven thousand cubic metres, and to an approximate diameter of fifty-seven metres.

"From the foregoing facts we are led to conclude that, since the chemical composition of the bolide is known, there must either exist huge cavities in the metal of the nucleus, or, which is more probable, the metal must be in a pulverulent state, the nucleus having a porous texture similar to that of a sponge.

"However this may be, our calculations and observations permit us to determine with approximate precision the value of the bolide. According to the present price of gold, this value is not inferior to two hundred and thirty-one thousand, five hundred and twenty millions sterling."

So, if the diameter was not a hundred metres, as the *Whaston Evening* had supposed, it was a good deal more than the ten metres assumed by the *Standard*. The truth was between the two hypotheses. As it was, there was enough to satisfy the desires of the covetous, had not the meteor been destined to go on its eternal round above the terrestrial globe.

When Mr. Dean Forsyth learnt the value of his bolide he cried:

"Seeing I have discovered it, and not the rascal in Morris Street, it belongs to me; and, if it should fall on the earth, all this wealth would be mine!"

On his side, Dr. Hudelson said, as he shook his fist in the direction of Elizabeth Street:

"It's my property, my children's inheritance, which is circling in space. If it should fall on our globe, no one could take it from me, and I should be fabulously rich!"

In sooth, the Vanderbilts, Astors, Rockefellers, Pierpont Morgans, Mackays, Goulds, and other American Crœsuses, not to speak of the Rothschilds, would look small beside Dr. Hudelson and Mr. Dean Forsyth, in case their claims were collectively or respectively admitted. It was enough to turn their heads!

Francis and Mrs. Hudelson foresaw only too plainly whither events were leading. But how could they restrain the two rivals now that the matter had gone so far? Conversation on the subject was impossible with either. Both seemed to have forgotten the projected marriage, and thought of nothing but their dispute so foolishly fostered by the newspapers of the town.

The articles, usually so pacific, grew bitter; regrettable personalities were introduced, and threatened to set every one at loggerheads; and *Punch*, with its epigrams and caricatures, did not cease exciting the two adversaries. If it did not throw oil on the fire, it threw at least the salt of its wit, which made the fire crackle. Things came at length to such a pass that fears were entertained of the two astronomers' having recourse to a duel to settle their quarrel. A nice prospect for the two betrothed!

Happily for the public peace, while the astronomers were becoming madder, people elsewhere began to reflect that, since the bolide was not going to fall, there was little to be gained by raving about its value. No one could reach it any more than they could reach the moon. At each of its revolutions it reappeared exactly in the part of the heavens calculated. Its velocity was uniform; and, as the *Whaston Standard* had remarked in the beginning, there was no apparent reason why it should ever decrease. Such considerations, reproduced by the Press everywhere, contributed to allay the excitement. And, from that moment, less and less attention was paid to the bolide, a sigh or two of regret, none the less, escaping towards the elusive meteor.

In its issue of the 9th of May, *Punch* dwelt upon the growing indifference of the public to a phenomenon that had so recently been in the mouths and minds of all; and, prolonging its jokes, again fell foul of the two discoverers.

"How long," cried *Punch* indignantly, at the end of its article, "are the two malefactors to remain unpunished whom we have already held up to scorn? Not content with desiring to annihilate at one blow the city in which they were born, they are now causing the ruin of the most respectable families. Only last week one of our friends, deceived by their fallacious and lying allegations, squandered a large patrimony in less than two days. The unfortunate man had counted on the milliards to be yielded by the bolide. What will become of the poor children of our friend now that the milliards are proved to be . . . castles in the air! Need we add that this friend is symbolical, that his name is legion? We propose that all the inhabitants of the globe shall bring an action, with common accord, against Mr. Dean Forsyth and Dr. Sydney Hudelson, claiming damages of exactly the same amount as the value of the bolide. And we hope that payment will be enforced to the last cent!"

The two culprits, luckily, continued in ignorance of the threat. While the rest of their fellow-creatures returned to the contemplation of mundane things, they still soared in the azure, and still explored its depths with the object-glasses of their telescopes.

X

In which Zephyrin Xirdal has an idea, and even two.

IN familiar language people said: "Zephyrin Xirdal? . . . What an odd fellow!" Truly, both in mind and in body, Zephyrin Xirdal was something out of the ordinary.

Lanky and awkward, his shirt often collarless and always cuffless, his trousers like a corkscrew, his waistcoat minus several of its buttons, the pockets of his huge coat stuffed with a variety of objects, all his clothing, in fine, dingy and dirty, and made up out of the most incongruous costumes—such was Zephyrin Xirdal's outer man, and such was the manner in which he understood elegance. From his shoulders, bent and curved like the ceiling of a cellar, hung kilometric arms terminated by enormous hairy hands—dexterous in the extreme—which their owner washed only at very irregular intervals. His face was strikingly ugly—yet more striking than it was ugly: heavy, square chin, large, thick-lipped mouth with splendid teeth, broad, flat nose, protruding, badly-hemmed ears, in short, the antithesis of an Antinoüs countenance. As a set-off, however, there was a grandly modelled brow crowning this strange visage, like a temple crowning a hill, a temple hewn out of sublime thoughts. Last of all, to complete the beholder's amazement, Zephyrin Xirdal's soul looked out, beneath this forehead, from two prominent eyes which expressed, according to the hour and minute, either the most marvellous intelligence or the crassest stupidity.

Mentally the contrast was just as great between him and the rest of his fellows. Refractory to any regular education, he had resolved at an early age that he would instruct himself alone; and his parents had been compelled to yield to his indomitable will. On the whole the result was not bad. At an age when most boys are still at school, Zephyrin Xirdal had passed competitive examinations—to amuse himself, so he said—allowing him to enter first one and then another of the special higher University schools; and in these examinations he had always obtained the first place. However, such successes were not of much use to him, since he seemed to forget them; and, forgetting also to attend the classes in these various institutions, he was soon struck off the roll.

At eighteen he inherited, through the death of his parents, an income of some fifteen thousand francs; and, having given his signature to all the necessary papers laid before him by his uncle—as he called him—the banker, Robert Lecœur, whose real relation towards him was that of godfather and guardian, he installed himself in two small rooms on the sixth story of a house in the Rue Cassette, Paris. There he still lived at the age of thirty-one.

Since he had taken up his residence in this small flat, a multitude of things had gradually been heaped up in its two rooms, which, unfortunately, did not grow in size to receive them. Pell-mell stood or lay machines and electric piles, dynamos, optical instruments, retorts, and a hundred other heterogeneous apparatuses. Pyramids of brochures, books, and papers rose from the floor to the ceiling, mounting on the only chair there was and on the table, the height of which they simultaneously raised, so that our original did not notice the change, when, seated on the one, he wrote on the other. Moreover, when he found himself too much incommoded by the mass of papers, he remedied the inconvenience by sending a few of the bundles flying across the room by an energetic backhander; then, with his mind at rest, he sat down to work at a perfectly tidy table, since it was cleared and ready, in consequence, for future invasions.

What did Zephyrin Xirdal do? It must be owned that, as a rule, he contented himself with pursuing his dreams amidst the fragrant fumes of an ever-lighted pipe. But, now and again, at variable intervals, he had an idea. On that day he arranged his table in his own way, that is to say, by sweeping everything off it, and sat down and did not quit his seat until he had finished his task, whether the task lasted forty minutes or forty hours. Then, when the final point was attained, he left the paper containing the result of his researches on the table, where the said paper acted as a bait to catch a fresh pile, which, in turn, would be swept off, like its predecessor, on the occasion of a new spell of work.

In the course of these irregular fits of study he had dabbled in everything. Transcendental mathematics, physics, chemistry, physiology, philosophy, pure and applied science of one kind and another had successively solicited his attention. Whatever the problem was, he had always tackled it with the same impetuosity and frenzy, and had never abandoned it until it was solved, unless . . . unless another idea lured him away from it, with a like suddenness. Then it might happen that this out-and-out oddity would rush into the realms of fancy, pursuing the second butterfly whose bright colours fascinated him, and would completely forget his anterior preoccupations in the intoxication of his later dream.

But in such a case it was only an adjournment. Some fine day, suddenly coming across the work that he had begun, he would set to it again with fresh ardour, and, in spite, perhaps, of fresh interruptions, would not fail to bring it to a conclusion.

How many profound or ingenious insights, how many definitive notes on the most difficult points of exact or experimental science, how many practical inventions lay dormant in the heap of papers that Zephyrin Xirdal spurned with his foot! Never had he thought of profiting by these treasures, save when one of his few friends complained in his presence of the uselessness of a research in any direction whatever.

"Wait a bit," then said Xirdal. "I must have something bearing on the subject."

At the same time he stretched out his hand, plunged it amid the hundreds of crumpled sheets that lay near him, drew forth, without even making a mistake, the brochure treating of the subject mentioned, and presented it to his friend with permission to use it as he pleased. Not once did the idea enter his head that in so doing he was acting contrary to his own interests.

Money? What should he do with it? When he wanted any money he called on his godfather, Monsieur Robert Lecœur. If this gentleman had ceased to be his guardian, he remained his banker; and Xirdal was sure of returning from his visit with a sum that he spent to the last sou. Since he had been in the Rue Cassette, he had always proceeded in this manner to his entire satisfaction. To have continually fresh desires and to be able to realize them is evidently one form of happiness. It is not the only one. Without the shadow of the least desire, Zephyrin Xirdal was perfectly happy.

On the morning of the 10th of May, this happy man was comfortably sitting on his single chair, his feet resting, an inch or two higher than his head, on the window-bar, and was smoking a particularly agreeable pipe, while amusing himself in deciphering some rebuses and square words printed on a paper bag which his grocer had sent him with some eatable or other inside. When this important occupation was terminated, and the solution of the riddles found, he threw the bag on to the heap of papers and nonchalantly extended his left hand towards the table, with a vague notion of picking up anything that might be lying there.

What his left hand lighted on was a bundle of folded newspapers. Zephyrin took the first that came, which happened to be a week-old *Journal.* This antiquity did not repel a reader that lived outside of space and time. He therefore glanced over the first page, but, of course, did not read it. In the same way he glanced over the second and third, until he reached the end. On the last advertisement page he found some things that amused him, and, having paused a moment to look at them, he turned the paper, imagining he was reading another fresh page, whereas he had returned to the first one. Musingly his eyes wandered down the leading article, and all at once a flash of intelligence lighted up in them, which before had expressed the most complete absence of that quality. As he went on reading the flash became a blaze:

"Well! . . . Well! . . . Well! . . ." murmured Zephyrin Xirdal in three different tones, meanwhile proceeding to re-peruse the article.

He was accustomed to speak aloud in the solitude of his room. He even spoke often in the plural, in order, no doubt, to flatter himself that some audience or other was listening, an imaginary audience that could not fail of being numerous, since it comprised all the pupils, admirers, and friends that Zephyrin Xirdal had never had and never would have. On this occasion he was less eloquent and limited himself to his triple exclamation. Exceedingly interested by the *Journal's* article, he pursued his reading in silence.

What was it that had caught his attention? Simply this. The last person in the universe to discover the Whaston bolide, he, at the same time, learnt its strange composition, which the article before him was relating.

"Well! this is a joke! . . ." he said to himself, when he had finished his second perusal.

For a few minutes he remained buried in his thoughts; then he lifted his feet off the window-bar and approached the table. The working fit was imminent. Unhesitatingly he put his hand on the scientific review he was seeking, and, tearing off the band, opened the review at the very page he wanted.

A scientific review has the right to be more technical than a great daily. This particular review was no exception to the rule. The elements of the bolide—trajectory, velocity, volume, mass, nature—were given in a few words only, after pages of learned curves and algebraic equations. Zephyrin Xirdal assimilated without effort this intellectual nourishment, though it was somewhat hard of digestion, and next glanced at the sky, whose azure was without a stain.

" Ah ! we will have a look ! . . ." he murmured, after a few impatient calculations.

Dipping his arm beneath a heap of papers in one of the corners of the room, he sent them flying with a movement due to long habit.

" It's astonishing how easily I find things," he remarked to himself with satisfaction, as he uncovered an astronomical telescope which was coated with a layer of dust like that on a bottle of port a hundred years old.

In a few seconds he had placed the telescope in front of the window and was pointing it towards the part of the sky that he had determined by his calculations. Placing himself in front of the object-glass, he gazed for some minutes.

" It's quite true ! " was his sole comment.

Then, after brief reflection, he deliberately took down his hat and walked down his six flights of stairs with intent to go to the Rue Drouot and Monsieur Lecœur's bank, which was one of the glories of the said street.

Zephyrin Xirdal knew only one manner of doing his errands. He used neither omnibus, nor tramcar, nor cab. However far he had to go, he always went on foot. But even in this exercise—the most natural and the most practical of outdoor amusements—he must needs be original. With downcast eyes, and lurching with his broad shoulders to the right and to the left, he walked through the town as if he had been in a desert. Both vehicles and pedestrians he ignored with the like serenity. Consequently he was greeted with a number of ill-sounding epithets—clown! fool! bumpkin!—hurled at him by people he had knocked against, or on whose corns he had trodden. And with cabbies it was worse still, when they were obliged to stop their horses in order to avoid running over him; the language they used was really shocking. However, he did not care. In fact, he didn't hear the maledictions that rose behind him like the waves in a ship's wake; and imperturbably he continued his promenade, with long, powerful strides. Twenty minutes sufficed to bring him to the Rue Drouot and Lecœur's bank.

"Is my uncle in?" he asked of the porter, who rose at his entrance.

"Yes, Monsieur Xirdal."

"Is he alone?"

"Yes."

Zephyrin pushed the padded door and stalked into the room.

"Hallo! you here?" said the banker in an interrogative tone.

"Since you see me here in flesh and blood," replied Zephyrin, "I may remark that your question is an idle one and that an answer would be supererogatory."

Accustomed to his godson's singularities, Monsieur Lecœur laughed good-humouredly.

"That's so," he acquiesced. "Yet you might have said yes more simply. And may I ask the object of your visit?"

"You may, for . . ."

"After all, it's useless," interrupted Monsieur Lecœur. "My second question is as superfluous as the first, experience having proved to me that I never see you except when you want money."

"But," objected Zephyrin, "are you not my banker?"

"True," said Monsieur Lecœur, "yet confess you are a singular client? Will you allow me to give you a piece of advice?"

"By all means, if you wish."

"Well, my advice to you is to be not so economical. Deuce take it, my dear friend, what are you doing with your youth? Have you any notion of how your account stands with me?"

"Not the least."

"It's monstrous, simply, is your account. Why! your parents left you an income of fifteen thousand francs a year, and you don't manage to spend four thousand."

"Bah! . . ." exclaimed Xirdal, appearing surprised, though he had heard the same remark at least twenty times before.

"It's true. So your interest is accumulating. I don't know exactly what your present credit is, but it must be more than a hundred thousand francs. What's to be done with this money?"

"I will study the question," declared Zephyrin quite seriously. "However, if the money inconveniences you, you have only to get rid of it."

"How?"

"Give it away. The thing is simple enough."

"To whom?"

"To anybody. What is it to do with me?"

Monsieur Lecœur shrugged his shoulders.

"Well! what do you want to-day?" he asked. "Two hundred francs, as usual?"

"Ten thousand francs," replied Zephyrin.

"Ten thousand francs!" repeated the banker in surprise. "You are taking my advice with a vengeance. What do you want to do with these ten thousand francs?"

"Travel."

"An excellent idea. In what country?"

"I don't know."

Monsieur Lecœur, much amused, looked slily at his godson and client.

"It's a fine country," he answered seriously. "Here are your ten thousand francs. Is that all you want?"

"No," said Zephyrin. "I must also have a piece of land."

"A piece of land?" repeated the banker, more and more astonished. "What land?"

"A piece of land like any other; two or three square kilometres, about."

"That's small," replied Monsieur Lecoeur ironically. "Must it be in the Boulevard des Italiens?"

"No, not in France."

"Where, then?"

"I don't know," said Zephyrin coolly.

Monsieur Lecœur had difficulty in refraining from laughing.

"Anyway, you have a good deal of choice, then," he said. "But, tell me, my dear Zephyrin, aren't you just a little . . . cracked? What are you driving at? Tell me."

"I have some business in view," declared Zephyrin, while his forehead wrinkled under the weight of his reflections.

"Some business!" cried the banker, amazed.

That this funny fellow should be dreaming of business was enough to fill anybody with stupefaction.

"Yes," affirmed the visitor.

"Important?"

"Pooh!" replied Zephyrin. "An affair of five or six thousand milliards of francs."

At present the banker gazed at his godson with real anxiety. If the young man were not joking, he was mad, downright mad.

"What?" he asked.

"Between five and six thousand milliards of francs," repeated Zephyrin quietly.

"Are you in your senses, Zephyrin?" insisted Monsieur Lecœur. "Do you know that there is not enough gold on the earth to make-up even a hundredth of this fabulous sum?"

"On the earth, perhaps not," said Xirdal. "Elsewhere, yes."

"Elsewhere? . . ."

"Yes. Four hundred kilometres from here, according to the vertical."

A ray of light flitted across the banker's mind. Having learnt, like everybody else, from the papers what had occurred, he now thought he understood; and he was right.

"The bolide?" he said, his face growing a shade paler.

"Yes, the bolide," replied Xirdal calmly.

If any one else but his godson had come to speak to him of this phenomenon, he would have at once shown him the door. A banker's time is too precious to be wasted in listening to people who have lost their senses. But Zephyrin Xirdal

"You are thinking of exploiting the Bolide"

was not quite in this category. Although his brain was in a manner cracked, it none the less contained genius, to which nothing was *a priori* impossible.

"You are thinking of exploiting the bolide," asked Monsieur Lecœur, looking his godson square in the face.

"Why not? What is there extraordinary in that?"

"But this bolide is four hundred kilometres from the earth's surface; you have just said so. You don't claim, I imagine, to be able to raise yourself as far as that?"

"There is no need, if I make it fall."

"By what means?"

"I have got the means, and that's enough."

"You've got the means! . . . You've got the means! . . . How will you act on a body so far away? Where will you place your fulcrum? What force will you employ?"

"It would take too long to explain all that to you," answered Zephyrin. "And, what is more, it would be useless. You wouldn't understand."

"You are flattering!" retorted Monsieur Lecœur, yet without being the least vexed.

At his reiterated request, however, his godson consented to enter into a few brief explanations, which the narrator of this story will further abridge, premising that, in spite of his well-known taste for hazardous speculations, he has no intention of pronouncing upon these uninteresting theories, which are perhaps a trifle too bold.

For Zephyrin Xirdal, matter is only an appearance. It has no real existence. He claimed to prove this by the incapacity of any one's imagining its intimate constitution. Whether matter be decomposed into molecules, atoms, or particles, there will still remain a last fraction insoluble by any analysis, and the same difficulty will always be offered until a first principle is admitted which is not matter. This first immaterial principle is energy.

What is energy? Zephyrin Xirdal owned that he did not know. Man being in relation with the outside world only through his senses, and man's senses being affected only by things of the material order, all that is not matter remains a secret to him. If, through an effort of reason, he is able to admit the existence of an immaterial world, he is utterly incapable of conceiving its nature, for want of terms of comparison. And this will be the case as long as humanity shall not have acquired new senses, the latter not being *a priori* impossible of acquisition.

Whatever may be the truth with regard to this point, energy, according to Zephyrin Xirdal, fills the universe, and eternally oscillates between two limits—absolute equilibrium, which could only be obtained by its uniform distribution throughout space, and absolute concentration in one spot, which, in this case, would be surrounded with a perfect vacuum. Space being infinite, these two limits are equally inaccessible. The result is that immanent energy is in a state of perpetual kineticism. Since material bodies absorb energy unceasingly, and this concentration necessarily provokes elsewhere a relative nothingness, matter radiates, correspondingly, throughout space the energy it holds imprisoned.

Consequently, in opposition to the classical axiom: "nothing is created and nothing is destroyed," Zephyrin Xirdal proclaimed that there is continual creation and destruction. Substance being eternally destroyed is eternally re-composed. Each of its changes of state is accompanied with a radiation of energy and a corresponding destruction of substance. If this destruction cannot be detected by our instruments, the reason is that they are imperfect, an enormous quantity of energy being enclosed in an imponderable particle of matter, which, in Zephyrin Xirdal's opinion, explains why the stars are separated by such prodigious distances compared with their mediocre size.

The destruction, though not detected, nevertheless takes place. Sound, heat, electricity, light furnish indirect proofs of this. These phenomena are radiated matter, and through them energy, when liberated, manifests itself, albeit in a form as yet rudimentary and semi-material.

Pure energy, so to speak, sublimated, can only exist beyond the confines of our material worlds. It envelops these worlds with a *dynamo-sphere* in a state of tension directly proportional to their mass and diminishing with the distance from their surface. The manifestation of this energy and of its tendency to an ever greater condensation is attraction.

Such was the theory which Zephyrin Xirdal set before Monsieur Lecœur, who was slightly bewildered.

"Thus much being settled," concluded the speaker, as if he had been talking of the simplest things in the world, "it suffices for me to liberate a small quantity of energy, and to direct it towards any spot in space I choose, and I am able to influence a body near this spot, especially if the said body is of small importance, that is to say, if it does not contain very much energy. The problem is an exceedingly simple one!"

"And have you the means to liberate the energy?" asked the banker.

"I have what comes to the same thing, viz. the means to open a way for it, by removing from its path all that is substance and matter."

"Why, then!" exclaimed Monsieur Lecœur, "you might derange the whole of the celestial mechanism!"

Zephyrin Xirdal did not appear taken aback by the enormity of this hypothesis.

"At present," he said, with modest simplicity, "the machine I have constructed can give me only results that are much smaller. It is, however, quite powerful enough to influence a petty bolide of a few thousands tons' weight."

"Let's hope it will!" declared the banker, who was beginning to be persuaded. "But where do you intend to make the bolide fall?"

"On my land."

"What land?"

"The land you are going to buy for me, when I have effected the necessary computations. I will write to you on the subject. Of course, I will choose, as far as possible, an almost desert region, where the ground has little or no value. By the way, you will probably have difficulties in negotiating the deed of sale. I am not altogether free in my selection, and it may happen that the country will not be easy of access."

"You can leave that to me," said the banker. "It's for cases of difficulty that the telegraph has been invented. I will guarantee that everything is all right on that score."

Provided with this assurance and with the ten thousand francs, Zephyrin returned home as hastily as he had come, and at once sat down to his table, which he previously cleared by a backhander, as was his wont. The working fit was evidently at its maximum. All night he pored over his figures and diagrams, and in the morning the solution was reached. He had calculated the force required to be applied against the bolide, the length of time during which the application would have to be made, the directions which would have to be given to the force, and, finally, the place and time at which the bolide would drop. Straightway he seized his pen, wrote the promised letter to Monsieur Lecœur, ran downstairs and posted it, and ran up again and shut himself up once more in his room.

As soon as he had closed the door he went to one of the corners of the chamber—the one into which, the evening before, he had flung with such remarkable dexterity the bundle of papers that had previously hidden the telescope. Now it was necessary to perform the inverse operation. Xirdal, therefore, slipped his arm under the said heap, and, with a clever jerk, sent it back flying to the place from which it had come. This second feat brought to light a sort of dark-coloured box, which Zephyrin lifted without apparent effort and transported to the middle of the room, opposite the window.

The box looked quite an ordinary one, a simple cube of wood painted in a dark neutral tint. Inside there were numerous bobbins, intercalated in a series of glass bulbs, whose slender extremities were joined in twos with copper wires of progressively finer thickness. Above the box, in the open air, one could see, fixed on a peg in the focus of a metallic reflector, a last bulb, fusiform at each end, which no material conductor joined to the others.

By the aid of precise instruments Zephyrin placed the metallic reflector in the exact direction indicated to him by his calculations of the night before; then, having seen that everything was in order, he put into the lower part of the box a small tube which shone most brilliantly. While so engaged, he spoke, according to his custom, as if he were trying to get an imposing audience to admire his eloquence.

"This, gentlemen," he said, "is Xirdalium, a body a hundred times more radio-active than radium. I am willing to own to you that, if I utilize this body, it is more for show. Not that it is deleterious; but the earth radiates enough energy for me to do without adding more. It is a grain of salt thrown into the sea. Still, a little display is not unbecoming, methinks, in an experiment of this nature."

Whilst talking, he had shut the box, and now joined it by two cables to the elements of a pile placed on a dresser.

"Neuter-heliocoidal currents, gentlemen," he resumed, "have naturally, since they are neutral, the property of repelling all bodies without exception, whether these bodies be electrified positively or negatively. On the other hand, being heliocoidal, they commonly choose a heliocoidal form ; a child might understand that. . . . All the same, it's very lucky that I thought of discovering them. . . . How everything serves in life ! "

The electric circuit having been closed, a soft buzz was heard in the box, and a bluish light flashed from the bulb which was fixed on the peg. Almost immediately this bulb assumed a gyratory motion, which, beginning slowly, grew more rapid at each second, ultimately reaching a lightning speed. For a few moments Zephyrin Xirdal gazed at the bulb performing its mad waltz, then his eyes, looking in a direction parallel to the axis of the reflector, lost themselves in space.

At first sight there was nothing of a material character that showed the machine was producing any effect. However, an attentive observer might have remarked a phenomenon which, though manifesting itself unostentatiously, was, nevertheless, somewhat singular. The particles of dust that were held suspended in the air, seemed unable, when they came into contact with the edges of the metallic reflector, to trespass beyond this limit, and whirled about with violence and tumult as if hurtling against some invisible obstacle. In their aggregate these particles of dust formed a truncated cone, the base of which rested on the circumference of the reflector. Two or three yards away from the machine this cone, made up of impalpable, eddying particles, changed gradually into a cylinder an inch or two in diameter, and the cylinder of dust held together in the outside air, in spite of rather a fresh breeze, until it disappeared in the distance.

"I beg to announce to you, gentlemen, that everything is going on well," said Zephyrin Xirdal, sitting down on his unique chair and carefully filling his pipe.

Half an hour later he stopped his machine, but started it again several times during the day; on the morrow and for nineteen days he repeated his experiments, choosing for each of them a point of space slightly different from the preceding, when fixing the direction of his reflector.

On the twentieth day he had just started his machine once more, and had lighted his faithful pipe, when the demon of invention again seized on his mind. One of the consequences of his theory concerning the perpetual destruction of matter suddenly occurred to him; and at once, as was generally the case with him, he had conceived the principle of an electric pile susceptible of renewing itself by successive reactions, the last of which would restore decomposed bodies to their primitive state, Such a pile would evidently go on working until the total disappearance of the substances employed and until their entire transformation into energy. Practically, it was perpetual motion.

"Well! . . . Well! . . ." muttered Zephyrin excitedly.

He reflected, as he knew how to reflect, by projecting all the vital force of his being on to one point and in a single mass. This concentrated thinking which he caused to play round the dark parts of a problem was like a luminous beam in which all the sun's rays should be united.

"No objections," he said at last, translating aloud the result of his inward effort. "We must try that forthwith."

Taking his hat, Zephyrin Xirdal hopped down his six flights of stairs and hastened to the workshop of a small joiner who lived across the street. There, in a few words, he explained what he wanted, a sort of wheel mounted on an iron axle, and provided with twenty-seven little troughs round its rim. He gave the dimensions of the troughs, which were to be constructed so as to allow the jars that would fill them to remain vertical during the wheel's rotation. Having completed his explanations, and ordered the wheel to be made without delay, he proceeded a little farther to a druggist's, where he was well known. There he selected his twenty-seven jars, which the assistant packed up in stiff paper and tied round with thick string, affixing a small and convenient wooden handle.

This operation being performed, Zephyrin was about to return home with his parcel when, at the shop door, he met one of his few friends, a bacteriologist of real value. Absorbed in his thoughts, Xirdal did not see the bacteriologist; but the bacteriologist saw him.

"Hallo, Xirdal!" the friend cried, smiling. "Who would have expected to meet you?"

At this familiar voice the person addressed consented to bring his gaze back into the exterior world.

"Hallo!" he echoed; "why, it's Marcel Leroux!"

"Yes, it's me!"

"And how are you? I'm downright glad to see you."

"Well, I'm just off by train. As you see me, with this bag strapped on my shoulders, containing three pocket-handkerchiefs and several other articles of necessity, I am on my way to the seaside, where I intend to revel in the fresh air for a week."

"Lucky dog!"

"Why not imitate my example? I dare say there will be room for the couple of us in the train."

"That's so! . . ." began Zephyrin.

"Unless you have anything that keeps you in Paris just now," added the friend.

"No!"

"Nothing in particular? . . . no experiment that you're making?"

Xirdal tried to remember, but his memory failed him.

K

"No, nothing," he replied.

"In that case, let yourself be tempted. A week's holiday will do you a lot of good. And what long confabs we'll have on the sands! . . ."

"Not to speak," interrupted Zephyrin, "of the opportunity it will afford me to study a point that has been bothering me in connection with the question of tides. To some extent it is related to some general problems I am studying at present. I was just thinking about them when I met you," he added, with touching sincerity.

"Then you will come."

"Yes."

"Let's be jogging, then! . . . But I was forgetting. You will have to return home first, and I am not sure whether the train . . ."

"Oh! there's no need," replied Zephyrin. "I've got all I want here."

The absent-minded fellow pointed to his parcel of jars.

"All right," said Marcel Leroux merrily.

And the two friends strode off together in the direction of the station.

"You understand, I suppose, my dear Leroux, that the superficial tension . . ."

A couple they met forced the two companions to separate, and the rest of the sentence was lost in the noise of vehicles. But this did not trouble Xirdal, who imperturbably continued his demonstration, addressing himself successively to a series of passers-by, to their great surprise. The speaker took no notice, and went on discoursing while ploughing his way through the waves of people. And, in the meantime, as Xirdal, mounted on his new hobby, was hurrying towards the train that should carry him far from the city, there, in the Rue Cassette, up in a room of the sixth story, a dark yet harmless-looking box went on softly buzzing, and a metallic reflector still projected its bluish light, and the cylinder of eddying dust particles still travelled, slender but rigid, into the unknown depths of space.

Left to itself, the machine that Zephyrin Xirdal had neglected to stop, and whose existence even he had forgotten, proceeded with its obscure and mysterious task.

XI

In which Mr. Dean Forsyth and Dr. Hudelson experience a violent emotion.

AT present everybody was familiar with the bolide. In thought, at least, they had gone all round it. Its orbit, velocity, volume, mass, nature, and value were each determined. It had ceased to cause anxiety since, moving with uniform speed along its trajectory, it was destined never to fall upon the earth's surface. Nothing was, therefore, more inevitable than that the public should lose their interest in this inaccessible meteor, which was henceforth commonplace.

True, in the various observatories, some astronomers from time to time glanced at the golden sphere that circled above their heads; but they quickly turned away from it to attend to other problems. The earth possessed a second satellite. That was all. To savants who regard the world mostly as a mathematical abstraction, what did it matter whether this satellite was made of iron or of gold?

It was regrettable the minds of Mr. Dean Forsyth and Dr. Hudelson were not as ingenuous. The indifference that prevailed around them did not calm their fevered imaginations, and they carried on their observations of the bolide—their bolide—with ever the same ardour and frenzy. Each time it passed they were at their posts, gazing through their telescopes, even at hours when the meteor was only a few degrees above the horizon.

The splendid weather encouraged their mania, permitting them to perceive the bolide a dozen times in the twenty-four hours. Whether it were to fall on the earth or not, its peculiarities, rendering it eternally celebrated, increased their vain desire to be considered its sole discoverer. Under such circumstances, reconciliation was impossible between the two rivals, whose hatred of each other became bitterer every day. Both Mrs. Hudelson and Francis Gordon saw this only too plainly. The latter now was convinced that his uncle would do all in his power to oppose the wedding; and the former hardly dared to hope that her husband would yield at the last minute. To the despair of the engaged couple and Miss Loo's wrath, the marriage seemed, if not entirely doomed to be broken off, at least adjourned *sine die*.

And the situation, already so serious, was yet to be further complicated.

On the evening of the 11th of May Mr. Dean Forsyth, whose eye, as usual, was fixed on the object-glass of his telescope, quitted the instrument briskly, uttered a stifled exclamation, jotted down some hurried notes on a piece of paper, returned to his telescope, then left it again, and continued such to-and-fro behaviour until the bolide disappeared below the horizon. At this moment Mr. Dean was as pale as wax and breathed only with difficulty. Omicron, believing his master was ill, rushed towards him to help him. But the astronomer, repelling him, staggered down to his study, where he locked himself in. For more than thirty hours he stayed there without eating or drinking. Once during this period Francis succeeded in getting his uncle to open the door, but not sufficiently for himself to enter. And the astronomer looked so haggard that the young man was alarmed.

"What do you want with me?" Mr. Forsyth asked.

"You've been shut up for twenty-four hours, uncle," replied Francis; "let me bring you something to eat."

"I want nothing except quiet," said the astronomer, "and, if you wish to be of service to me, please do not disturb me again."

In presence of this attitude, and a tone at once so firm and mild, Francis could only obey. The door was locked again, and Francis sorrowfully withdrew. On the morning of the 13th of May, which was two days before that fixed for the marriage, the prospective bridegroom related to

Mrs. Hudelson this fresh occurrence, and spoke of the anxiety it caused him.

"I can't understand," she said, when he had finished. "It's enough to make one believe that both Mr. Forsyth and my husband are mad."

"What!" cried Francis. "Has something else happened with the doctor?"

"Yes," answered Mrs. Hudelson. "If your uncle and the doctor had been accomplices they could scarcely have acted with greater similarity. With my husband the fit came on a little later, that's all. It was only yesterday morning that he shut himself up in his study. Since then we haven't seen him, and you can imagine in what trouble we are."

"It's enough to drive us all crazy!" exclaimed Francis.

"What you tell me about Mr. Forsyth," resumed Mrs. Hudelson, "leads me to suppose that they have both noticed something fresh in connection with their stupid bolide. And I fear the worst from the state they are in."

"Ah! if I were only mistress! . . ." cried Loo.

"What should you do, my dear little sister?" asked Francis.

"What would I do? Something very simple. I would send this dreadful bolide flying so far, so far that the best telescopes should not see it."

Perhaps, indeed, the disappearance of the bolide might have restored Mr. Forsyth and Dr. Hudelson to a calmer condition of mind. And who knows if their absurd jealousy of each other would not have also disappeared? But it did not seem likely that this would come about. The bolide would be in its place on the wedding morning; it would be there the day after, and it would be there always, since it revolved with regular course up there in the heavens.

"Anyway," concluded Francis, "we shall see. In a couple of days they will have to decide, and we shall know what to do."

Returning to Elizabeth Street, he was encouraged to think that, after all, things might go well. Mr. Dean Forsyth had issued at length from his retirement and made a hearty, though silent, meal. Now, replete and tired out, he was fast asleep, while Omicron was in town on an errand for his master.

"Did you see my uncle before he went to bed?" Francis asked of Mitz.

"Yes, sonny, since I gave him his food."

"Was he hungry?"

"Ravenous. He swallowed everything: *rambled* eggs" (Mitz must have meant *rumbled*), "cold roast beef, potatoes, fruit, pudding. He ate it all."

"How did he seem?"

"Not too bad, except that he was as white as a *sceptre*, and his eyes all red. I advised him to bathe them with some *older* water; but he didn't appear to pay attention."

"Did he leave any message for me?"

"Neither for you nor for anybody. He *ate without opening his mouth*, and he went to lie down, after sending *My Crown* to the *Whaston Standard*."

"To the *Whaston Standard!*" cried Francis. "It's no doubt to communicate the result of the work he has been engaged on. So we shall have another newspaper controversy. And we've had enough already."

Francis was right. The next morning he was annoyed to read in the *Standard* his uncle's communication, which he was convinced would serve to envenom the relations of the two astronomers, and would further prejudice his own and Jenny's chances of happiness. His vexation was not diminished when he found that there was a similar communication from the doctor in the *Whaston Morning*. Similar in their opening statements, the two letters differed in their conclusions. The subject they treated was one indeed that not Whaston alone, but the world at large, was informed of at once through telegraph and telephone.

Mr. Dean Forsyth and Dr. Hudelson began by declaring that their constant observations of the bolide had enabled them to remark an evident perturbation in its movement. Its orbit, which had hitherto been due north-south, was at present slightly modified and lay north-east, south-west. On the other hand, a much more important modification had been discovered in its distance from the earth. At present the distance was sensibly less, without any corresponding increase of velocity. From these observations and the calculations based upon them, the two astronomers concluded that the meteor, instead of continuing in the same eternal orbit, would necessarily fall on the earth at some spot so far undeterminable exactly.

Up to this point Mr. Forsyth and the doctor agreed in their arguments. Beyond it they totally disagreed. Whereas the learned equations of the one induced him to predict that the bolide would fall on the 28th of June in the southern regions of Japan, the equally learned equations of the other led him to declare that the fall would take place only on the 7th of July in some part of Patagonia.

The public was free to choose! For the moment the public, however, could think of nothing else than the fact that the bolide was going to fall, and with it the thousands of milliards which it was bearing through space. This was the essential thing. For the rest, what did they care? The milliards would be found, wherever they might fall.

The consequences of such an event, the economic disturbance that so prodigious an afflux of gold could not fail to cause, formed the subject of all conversations. In general, the rich were in consternation, thinking of the probable depreciation of their fortunes. On the contrary, the poor were delighted by the prospect, fallacious as it might prove, of their having a share of the cake.

Francis was terribly upset. The milliards or billiards were nothing to him. All he wanted was his Jenny, a treasure infinitely more precious than those of the wretched bolide. He hurried to Morris Street, and found that they were already in possession of the melancholy news, and were speculating as to the effect it would produce upon their plans. Loo's rage knew no bounds. Jenny wept tears that neither her mother, sister, nor lover could dry up, though Francis swore that he would wait, if necessary, until the last cent of the milliards were spent by the one who should obtain the meteor. The oath was an imprudent one, since it appeared likely to condemn him to remain a bachelor all his life.

XII

In which Mrs. Arcadia Stanfort is seen to wait in her turn, not without much impatience, and in which Mr. John Proth declares himself not competent.

ON this particular morning Judge Proth was at his window, while his servant Kate was busying herself about the room. You may be sure that the judge troubled little whether the bolide passed or did not pass above Whaston. No; without preoccupations of any kind, he allowed his eyes to wander over Constitution Square, of which his window afforded a complete and excellent view.

But what the judge deemed of such small interest had a certain importance in Kate's eyes.

"So it's in gold, sir," Kate remarked, pausing close to her master.

"Apparently," answered the judge.

"You don't seem to be much affected, sir."

"That's true, Kate."

"And yet, sir, if it's in gold, it must be worth millions."

"Millions and milliards, Kate. Yes, there are milliards trotting round above our heads."

"And they are going to fall, sir."

"So people say."

"Just think, sir. There'll be no more poor folk on the earth."

"There'll be just as many, Kate."

"But, sir . . ."

"It would take too long to explain, Kate. Do you know how much a milliard is?"

"A milliard, sir . . . why it's . . . it's . . ."

"It's a thousand millions."

"As much as that!"

"Yes, Kate; and if you were to live a hundred years, you wouldn't have time to count a milliard, even if you were to devote ten hours a day to the task."

"Is it possible, sir?"

"Yes, it's certain."

The servant remained for a moment amazed at the thought that a century would not suffice to count a milliard! Then she resumed her work with broom and duster, stopping, however, now and again, as if overcome by her reflections.

"How much would it make for each person, sir?"

"What, Kate?"

"The bolide, sir, if it was shared alike among everybody."

"That would have to be calculated, Kate," answered the judge, and he took up a piece of paper and a pencil.

"Admitting," he said, as he ciphered, "that the earth contains fifteen hundred million inhabitants, that would make not quite seven hundred and fifteen dollars apiece."

"No more . . ." murmured Kate, disappointed.

"No more," declared Mr. Proth, while Kate looked at the sky musingly.

When she returned to a consideration of her surroundings, she perceived, at the bottom of Exeter Street, a couple of people to whom she drew her master's attention.

"Just look at those two ladies waiting there, sir," she said.

"Yes, Kate, I see them."

"Look at one of them . . . the taller . . . the one who is stamping her foot impatiently."

"You are right, Kate, she is stamping her foot. But I don't know who the lady is."

"Why, sir, she's the same who came and got married here two months ago on horseback."

"Miss Arcadia Walker?" asked the judge.

"Mrs. Stanfort now."

"You are right. It is the lady herself."

"What's she want here, I wonder?"

"I don't know," answered the judge; "and, what is more, I wouldn't give a farthing to learn."

"Can she be wanting our services again?"

"It's not likely, since bigamy is not allowed in the territories of the Union," said Mr. Proth, shutting the window. "Anyhow, I mustn't forget it's time to go to the court, where an important case comes on to-day, relating, as it happens, to the bolide that interests you so much. If this lady should call, you must express my regret at being unable to see her."

Whilst speaking, Mr. John Proth had made ready to go out. With tranquil step he went downstairs, quitted the house by the little door opening into Solomon Street, and disappeared inside the town Law Courts, which stood exactly opposite his house on the other side of the street.

The servant was not mistaken. It was, in fact, Mrs. Arcadia Stanfort who, on this particular morning, was in Whaston, with her chambermaid, Bertha. Both were impatiently walking to and fro, gazing from time to time up Exeter Street.

The town clock struck ten.

"To think he's not yet here!" cried Mrs. Arcadia.

"Perhaps he has forgotten the day of the appointment," suggested Bertha.

"Forgotten!" repeated the lady indignantly.

"Unless he has changed his mind," added Bertha.

"Changed his mind!" repeated her mistress still more indignantly.

She walked a few steps nearer to Exeter Street, with the chambermaid at her heels.

"Can't you see him?" she asked impatiently after a few moments.

"No, ma'am."

"It's too bad!"

Mrs. Stanfort returned towards the Square.

"Not yet here! . . . The idea of making me wait . . . after what was settled between us!" she said. "Tuesday is the 18th, I believe!"

"Yes, ma'am."

"And it will soon be half-past ten."

"In ten minutes."

"Well! he needn't imagine he will tire out my patience! I will wait here all day, if need be!"

The hotel servants of Constitution Square might have noticed the lady's behaviour, as they had noticed, a couple of months before, the impatience of the horseman who was watching to take her to the magistrate's house. But at present everybody—men, women, and children—was thinking of something else, something about which, in all Whaston, Mrs. Stanfort was the only person not to think. Everybody was taken up with the marvellous meteor, its revolutions in the firmament, its fall that was announced for a fixed date, albeit the date was differently predicted by the two astronomers of the town. The groups of people assembled on the Square paid little or no attention to Mrs. Stanfort's presence. We cannot say whether popular superstition is correct in attributing to the moon an influence upon the human brain. At any rate, we may state that our globe then contained a prodigious number of persons who might have been called *meteor-struck*. They forgot to eat and drink in thinking that a globe worth milliards was circling above their heads, and would before long come crashing down on the ground.

Mrs. Stanfort was evidently preoccupied with other cares.

"Can't you see him, Bertha?" she again said, after further waiting.

"No, ma'am."

At this moment cries arose at the end of the Square. Those who were walking by rushed to the place. Several hundreds of people had also come from neighbouring streets, so that the crowd was a large one. At the same instant the hotel windows of the Square exhibited their complement of inquisitive faces.

"There . . . see there! . . ." were the words that issued from every one's mouth. And Mrs. Stanfort, believing they referred to the gentleman she was expecting, exclaimed:

"At last he's coming."

"No, ma'am," said the chambermaid. "They are not shouting about us."

And in truth Mrs. Arcadia and her affairs were nothing to these people, who, with raised faces and gesticulating arms, were all looking towards the northern horizon. Was it the famous bolide, about to show itself above the town?

and had the inhabitants gathered to salute it on its journey? No. At this precise hour it was ploughing its way through the sky of the other hemisphere. Indeed, even if it had been above the Whaston horizon just now, no naked eye could have perceived it in the daytime. To whom or to what, then, were the crowd's acclamations addressed?

"It's a balloon, ma'am!" said Bertha. "Look! there it is behind Saint Andrew's spire."

Bertha was right. Slowly descending from the upper zones of the atmosphere, an aerostat appeared, greeted by the applause of the crowd. Why these shouts? Had the balloon ascent any particular interest? Were there special reasons why the public should accord it such a reception?

Yes, there were reasons. On the evening before, the balloon had ascended from a neighbouring town, carrying with it the celebrated aeronaut, Walter Wragg, and his assistant. This ascent had been made for the purpose of attempting an observation of the bolide under more favourable conditions. Such was the cause of the crowd's excitement, and of the anxiety—they wished to know the results of this original experiment.

Of course, as soon as the ascent was decided on, Mr. Dean Forsyth, to Mitz's great fright, had requested to be allowed to join the aeronaut; and, of course, Dr. Hudelson had claimed to have his place in the car, to the no less fright of his

"It's a balloon, ma'am"

wife. The situation was a delicate one, for the aeronaut had room only for one passenger. There was a lively dispute between the two astronomers, as may be supposed. Finally, both had been refused, and a third person was chosen, whom Mr. Walter Wragg asserted to need as his assistant, that he could not do without.

At present a gentle breeze was wafting the balloon towards the Square of Whaston, and the population prepared to give the two aeronauts a hearty welcome. Gradually and quietly the balloon descended and touched the ground, at last, exactly in the middle of the Square. A hundred hands immediately seized the car, out of which Mr. Walter Wragg and his assistant proceeded to extricate themselves. Leaving his principal to see to the deflation of the balloon, the latter advanced with rapid steps towards Mrs. Arcadia Stanfort. As soon as he was near enough to speak, he bowed and said:

"Here I am, madam."

"At ten thirty-five," replied the lady shortly, pointing to the town clock.

"And our appointment was for half-past ten, I know," acquiesced the new-comer politely. "I beg you will excuse me, since aerostats do not always obey our will as exactly as one would desire."

"So I am not mistaken," said the lady. "You were in the balloon with Walter Wragg."

" Yes, I was."

" Will you explain ? "

" Nothing is more simple. The thing seemed to me original. I meant to keep our appointment by arriving in this manner. I therefore induced Walter Wragg, by paying so many dollars down, to promise he would land me here this morning at half-past ten punctually. I think an error of five minutes may be pardoned him."

" It may," granted Mrs. Arcadia Stanfort, " since you have arrived. I presume your intentions have not changed ? "

" Not at all."

" Your opinion is still that we shall do wisely in giving up our life in common ? "

" Yes, such is my opinion."

" Mine is that we are not made for each other."

" I quite share your conviction."

" Still, Mr. Stanfort, I am quite ready to recognize your qualities."

" And yours I appreciate also."

" We may esteem each other and yet not please each other. Love and esteem are two different things. Esteem is not sufficient for such incompatibility of temperaments to be supported."

" What you say is most true."

" It is evident that if we had loved each other ! . . ."

" Things would be quite different."

" But we do not love each other."

" This is only too patent."

" We married without sufficiently knowing each other, and we have been mutually disappointed. . . . Ah ! if we had rendered each other some signal service, susceptible of striking our imaginations, the result might have been different."

" Unfortunately this has not been the case. You have not had to sacrifice your fortune to prevent me from being ruined."

" I would have done it, Mr. Stanfort. On your side, you have not had to save my life at the risk of your own."

" I should not have hesitated, Mrs. Arcadia."

" I am sure you would not. But the opportunity has never offered itself. We were strangers to each other, and strangers we have remained."

" This is deplorably accurate."

" We thought we had the same tastes, at least, as regards travelling . . ."

" And we have never been able to agree concerning the direction we would take ! "

" True ; when I wanted to go south, you wanted to go north."

" And when I wished to go west, you wished to go east."

" This bolide was the last straw."

" It was the drop that made the cup brim over."

" You are still determined to side with Mr. Dean Forsyth ? "

"Quite."

"And to start for Japan, to be present at the meteor's fall?"

"Yes."

"Well! I am as resolved on following the opinion of Dr. Sydney Hudelson . . ."

"And on going to Patagonia . . ."

"There is no conciliation possible."

"No, none."

"We have, therefore, only one course open to us."

"Yes."

"Namely, to appear before the judge."

"I am ready, madam."

Both turned and proceeded in single file, the lady in front, towards Mr. Proth's house. Bertha, the chambermaid, brought up the rear.

Old Kate was on the doorstep.

"Mr. Proth?" asked Mr. and Mrs. Stanfort simultaneously.

"He is out," replied Kate.

The faces of both applicants fell.

"Will he be long?" asked the lady.

"He won't be back till lunch," said Kate.

"At what time does he lunch?"

"At one o'clock."

"We will come back at one o'clock," declared Mr. and Mrs. Stanfort together, as they turned to go away.

Reaching the middle of the Square, which was

still cumbered with Walter Wragg's balloon, they paused for a moment.

"We have two hours to wait," said Mrs. Arcadia.

"Two hours and a quarter," corrected Mr. Seth Stanfort.

"Would it suit you for us to spend these two hours in each other's company?"

"If you will have the kindness to consent."

"What would you say to a sail on the Potomac?"

"I was about to make the same proposal."

Husband and wife had just begun to walk in the direction of Exeter Street when they stopped after a few steps.

"Will you allow me to make a remark?" asked the gentleman.

"Certainly."

"I should like to observe that we are in agreement for the first time."

"It is the last also," answered the lady.

In order to get to Exeter Street, Mr. and Mrs. Stanfort were obliged to thread their way through the crowd, which had become more dense around the aerostat. Indeed, they would have found it almost impossible to pass at all but for another attraction quite as sensational, if not more, which was tempting a large number of people to enter the Whaston Court of Justice. At an early hour in the morning people had been waiting for the doors to be opened; and, as soon as entrance was allowed, they had rushed in and filled the audience-room in the twinkling of an eye. Many had been turned away, unable to squeeze themselves in, and it was these for the most part who had supplied the spectators at the balloon's descent.

How much they would have preferred being packed with the privileged ones that were listening to the pleading of the most gigantic case that has ever been and ever will be submitted to a judge's decision!

Be it granted that popular excitement had been carried to its apparently extreme limits when the Paris Observatory published the news that the bolide, or at least the bolide's nucleus, was of pure gold. Yet this delirium was nothing to be compared with that which had been aroused when Mr. Dean Forsyth and Dr. Sydney Hudelson predicted that the asteroid would fall. Innumerable were the people who went mad on the occasion; and in a few days all the lunatic asylums were found to be too small for the patients that they had to accommodate.

But, among all these mad persons, assuredly the maddest were the authors of the excitement that was raging over the globe. Previously the two astronomers had competed with each other solely for the glory of giving their respective names to the bolide. After what they learnt during the night between the 11th and 12th of May, the chief dispute was as to which of them the bolide would belong when it fell.

"To me!" cried Mr. Dean Forsyth unhesitatingly. "To me, since I was the first to point out its existence above the Whaston horizon!"

"To me!" cried Dr. Hudelson with equal conviction, "since I really discovered it!"

These claims being contradictory and irreconcilable, the two foolish astronomers had not failed to have recourse to the Press to uphold them. For two days the Whaston papers were filled with the two adversaries' inflamed prose. Both correspondents abused each other to their hearts' content, while the bolide maintained its revolutions with the sublimest indifference.

As may be supposed, there could be no question of the marriage while things were like this. Consequently the 15th of May went by without Francis and Jenny's ceasing to be "the betrothed." Had they even the right to call themselves betrothed? To his nephew, who had tried once more to persuade him, Mr. Dean Forsyth replied:

"I consider the doctor a scoundrel, and I will never give my consent to your marriage with the daughter of a Hudelson."

Almost at the same hour the said Dr. Hudelson cut short his daughter's lamentations, and declared:

"Francis' uncle is a dishonest man; my daughter shall never marry the nephew of a Forsyth."

It was categoric. There was nothing left but submission.

Walter Wragg's balloon ascent had furnished fresh food to the two astronomers' animosity. In the letters published in the Press the adversaries used expressions of the most violent kind. Finally, since abuse decided nothing, appeal was made to the Court of Justice; and a summons had been issued to the two litigants to appear on the 18th of May, in the morning, before Judge Proth. Both arrived in due course and waited their turn to be called. After several minor cases had been disposed of satisfactorily, the clerk read out their names: Forsyth against Hudelson and Hudelson against Forsyth."

"Let the gentlemen come forward," said the judge, sitting up in his chair.

Mr. Dean Forsyth and the doctor advanced from the two groups of their partisans, with whom they had been talking. Now they were facing each other, with flashing eyes and clenched hands, like a couple of cannons loaded to the muzzle, that a spark would suffice to fire.

"What is the question in dispute, gentlemen?" asked Judge Proth, who knew perfectly well why the astronomers were before him.

"Mr. Dean Forsyth was the first to answer.

"I have come to uphold my rights . . ."

" And I mine . . ." interrupted Dr. Hudelson.

Thereupon a deafening duet was begun, in which all the rules of harmony were violated and nothing but dissonance was heard.

Mr. Proth rapped his desk with his ivory paper-knife, like the conductor of an orchestra who raps with his bow to stop an insupportable cacophony.

" Please, gentlemen, have the kindness to explain in turn. Proceeding in alphabetical order, I invite Mr. Forsyth to speak first; Dr. Hudelson will then reply."

Consequently Mr. Dean Forsyth proceeded to set forth his statement, while Dr. Hudelson listened and was compelled to bridle his anger. The former related how, on the 16th of March, at thirty-seven minutes, twenty seconds past seven, being posted at the summit of his tower in Elizabeth Street, he had perceived a bolide traversing the sky from north to south, how he had continued his observation of the meteor during all the time it had remained visible, and how he had sent a letter a few days later to the Pittsburg Observatory, for the purpose of drawing attention to his discovery and of laying claim to priority in the matter.

When Dr. Hudelson was in turn permitted to speak, he could only give an identical account, so that the Court, after hearing the two statements, was no further advanced than at the commencement. However, Mr. Proth forbore to ask for any supplementary information. Having, with a gesture, imposed silence, he gave his judgment, which he had prepared while the two adversaries were pleading.

"Considering, on the one hand," said the judgment, "that Mr. Dean Forsyth declares he discovered a bolide traversing the atmosphere above Whaston on the 16th of March, at thirty-seven minutes, twenty seconds past seven in the morning;

"Considering, on the other hand, that Dr. Sydney Hudelson declares he perceived the same bolide at the same hour, at the same minute, at the same second;"

"Yes! yes!" cried the doctor's adherents, shaking their fists in the air.

"No! no!" retorted Mr. Forsyth's adherents, stamping on the floor.

"But, whereas the case in dispute involves a question of minutes and seconds, and is of an exclusively scientific order;

"Whereas there exists no legal precedent applicable to the priority of an astronomic discovery;

"On these grounds, we declare that we are not competent to decide, and we mulct the two parties jointly in the costs."

The magistrate was evidently unable to make any other reply. And he hoped, no doubt, that, being non-suited in this manner, they would henceforth abstain from further recrimination. But neither the litigants nor their partisans were willing that the case should finish in this manner. If Mr. Proth thought that his plea of non-competence would have any such effect, he was mistaken. Two voices rose above the general murmurs that his decision had provoked.

"I claim the right to speak," cried Mr. Dean Forsyth and Dr. Hudelson together.

"Although I do not intend to reopen the case," replied the magistrate, in the amiable tone that he never abandoned, even under the gravest circumstances, "I am quite willing to allow both Mr. Forsyth and Dr. Hudelson to say a few words by way of conclusion, provided they will speak only one at a time."

This was too much to ask of the two rivals. They each began to perorate with the same volubility and vehemence, neither of them consenting to let the other gain a single syllable.

Judge Proth, believing it was his wisest plan to permit them to go on, paid what attention he could, and succeeded in learning that they now were debating the all-important question to them of their respective rights to the bolide whenever it should fall.

"It belongs to Mr. Forsyth," shouted the one side in chorus.

"It belongs to Dr. Hudelson," shouted the other.

Smiling philosophically, the magistrate at length obtained silence sufficient for him to pronounce a few words himself.

"Gentlemen," he said, "you will excuse my giving you a piece of advice. In case the bolide should fall . . ."

"It will fall!" clamoured the partisans on both sides.

"Very well!" acquiesced the obliging magistrate. "I see no objection, if only it does not fall on the flowers in my garden."

A few smiles appeared amongst the assembly. Mr. Proth profited by this to direct one of his most benevolent looks towards each of the disputants in turn. Alas! it was lost trouble. He might more easily have tamed two blood-thirsty tigers.

"In this case," resumed the fatherly magistrate, "since the bolide is of such value, I should advise you to go shares."

"Never."

All those present were unanimous in pronouncing this word. Never would Mr. Forsyth and Dr. Hudelson consent to split the difference. True, they would have each obtained nearly six hundred thousand millions of dollars; but what was this in comparison with a question of *amour-propre?* Being so intimately acquainted with human weaknesses, Mr. Proth was not over astonished that his advice, wise though it was, should meet with the assembly's disapprobation. He was by no means disconcerted and waited for the hubbub to cease.

"Since all conciliation is impossible," he said, as soon as he was able to make himself heard once more, "the Court will pronounce its judgment."

At these words a deep silence fell as if by magic, and, without the slightest interruption, the magistrate dictated the sentence to his clerk.

"The Court having heard the two parties further in their arguments and conclusions; and

"Whereas the allegations made are of equal weight on both sides and are supported by the same evidence;

"Whereas the discovery of a meteor does not necessarily confer a right of property over it, the law being mute on this question, and there being no precedent to go upon;

"Whereas the exercise of such pretended right of property might, by reason of the peculiar circumstances of the case, meet with insurmountable difficulties, and any judgment whatsoever would risk being a dead letter, which, to the great detriment of the principles whereon all civilised society reposes, would tend to diminish the authority of the law in the public mind;

"Whereas it behoves in so peculiar a case to act with prudence and circumspection;

"And whereas, in fine, the suit entered turns,

whatever the parties may urge, on a hypothetic event which may, after all, not occur;

"Since the meteor may fall in one of the seas that cover three parts of the globe;

"Since, then, the case would necessarily be struck off the roll, in consequence of the disappearance of the object in dispute;

"The Court, on these grounds, decides:

"To defer its verdict until after the duly proved fall of the bolide in question:

"Full stop," concluded Mr. Proth, rising at the same time from his chair.

The sitting was at an end. And the public were much impressed by the prudent considerations of the judge. As he had said, it was quite possible the bolide might fall into the sea, whence no one would be able to fish it up. Then there were the "insurmountable difficulties" at which he had hinted. What could these be? In fine, those who had been present went away in reflective mood, and thereby calmer than when they came.

Exception, however, must be made for the two litigants, who neither reflected nor grew calm. On the contrary, at the two ends of the room, they stood and excitedly harangued their partisans.

"I will not accept this judgment," yelled Mr. Dean Forsyth with stentorian voice. "It is ridiculous."

HAPPILY, THE AUTHORITIES HAD TAKEN THEIR PRECAUTIONS

"Absurd!" shouted Dr. Sydney Hudelson at the same moment.

"The idea of saying my bolide will not fall! . . ."

"The idea of doubting the fall of my bolide!"

"It will fall where I have predicted!"

"I have fixed the place where it will tumble!"

"And since I cannot get justice done! . . ."

"Since I am denied justice! . . ."

"I will go and defend my rights to the end. I will start this evening . . ."

"I will uphold my claim to the last extremity. This very day I will start . . ."

"For Japan!" cried Mr. Dean Forsyth.

"For Patagonia!" cried Dr. Hudelson.

"Hurrah!" responded the two camps with one voice.

When everybody was out in the street, the crowd formed itself into two groups, joined by the inquisitives who had not been able to obtain entrance into the court. The tumult increased. There were bawlings, challenges, threats on every side. And soon the affair would have degenerated into a free fight, for the partisans of Mr. Dean Forsyth were quite ready to lynch Dr. Hudelson, and the partisans of Dr. Hudelson were just as ready to lynch Mr. Dean Forsyth. Happily the authorities had taken their precautions. Numerous policemen intervened at this point and resolutely separated the combatants.

This was exactly what was required to assuage

their somewhat superficial passion. However, in order to have a pretext for making as much noise as possible, they exchanged their shouts against the adversary for cheers in honour of their respective favourites.

"Hurrah for Dean Forsyth!"

"Hurrah for Hudelson!"

These acclamations were thundered forth, and before long blended into a single roar.

"To the station!" bellowed both parties, at last in agreement.

The crowd immediately drew up in two processions, and so crossed Constitution Square, which was now disembarrassed of Walter Wragg's balloon. At the head of one of the processions marched Mr. Dean Forsyth, and at the head of the other Dr. Sydney Hudelson. The police did not interfere, seeing that there was no further disturbance to be feared. In fact, the two bodies of partisans diverged as soon as they left the Square, the crowd piloted by Mr. Dean Forsyth proceeding triumphantly towards the West Station, which was the point of departure for San Francisco and Japan, and the crowd piloted by Dr. Sydney Hudelson proceeding no less triumphantly to the East Station, the point of departure for New York, where the doctor could embark for Patagonia.

Gradually the shouts died away; and Mr. John Proth, who, from his doorstep, had been amusing himself with watching the noisy demonstrations of the throng of people, bethought himself that it was lunch time and turned to enter the house. At this moment he was accosted by a lady and gentleman who had reached his door by walking round the Square.

"A word, if you please, Judge," said the gentleman.

"At your service, Mr. and Mrs. Stanfort," replied Mr. Proth amiably.

"When we appeared before you two months ago, Mr. Proth," continued Seth Stanfort, "it was to get you to marry us."

"And I congratulate myself," said the judge, "that I was able to make your acquaintance on that occasion."

"To-day, sir," added Mr. Stanfort, "we have come to ask you to divorce us."

Judge Proth, being an experienced man, understood at once that it would be useless to attempt a reconciliation at this moment.

"Even so," he answered, "I congratulate myself on the opportunity you afford me of renewing my acquaintance with you."

The couple bowed.

"Will you kindly come in?" proposed the magistrate.

"Is it really necessary?" asked Mr. Seth Stanfort, as he had asked two months before.

And, as two months before, Mr. Proth replied phlegmatically:

"Not at all. Have you your papers in order?"

"Here are mine," said Mr. Stanfort.

"And here are mine," said Mrs. Stanfort.

Mr. Proth took the documents, examined them, assured himself that they were properly worded and all formalities complied with, after which he replied:

"Then here is the divorce ready printed. We have only to write your names and to have your signatures. But I am not sure that we can manage here . . ."

"Allow me to propose to you this improved stylograph pen," said Mr. Stanfort, holding out the said implement.

"And this case will serve very well as a pad," added Mrs. Stanfort, taking from her chambermaid's hands a large flat sort of box, which she offered to the magistrate.

"You have a way out of every difficulty," approved the latter, beginning to fill in the spaces.

When he had finished he presented the pen to Mrs. Stanfort. Without the least hesitation or the least trembling of her hand, she signed her name, Arcadia Walker. And, with the same coolness, Mr. Seth Stanfort signed his name after hers. Then each of them, as two months before, brought out a five hundred dollar note:

"Your fees," said Mr. Seth Stanfort again.

"For the poor," repeated Miss Arcadia Walker.

Straightway they bowed to the magistrate,

saluted each other, and departed, the one towards Wilcox suburb, the other in exactly the opposite direction. When they had disappeared, Mr. Proth entered the house, where lunch was waiting for him.

"Do you know, Kate, what I ought to put on the front of my house?" he asked the old servant, while he fixed his serviette under his chin.

"No, sir."

"I ought to put this: 'Here people marry on horseback and get divorced on foot!'"

XIII

In which, as was foreseen by Judge Proth, a third competitor appears, soon followed by a fourth.

IT is best we should not attempt to depict the grief of the Hudelson family and Francis Gordon. Certainly, had Francis been free in his actions, he would not have hesitated to break with his uncle, to brave the latter's anger and its consequences. But what he might have been able to do against Mr. Dean Forsyth's wishes he could not against Dr. Hudelson's. In vain had Mrs. Hudelson tried to obtain her husband's consent, and Loo had added her prayers, coaxings, and tears. Nothing had moved the obstinate doctor. And now both the uncle and the father had started for foreign parts.

Yet how useless this double departure was! How useless also the divorce of Mr. Seth Stanfort and Miss Arcadia Walker, determined by the two astronomers' affirmations. If these four people had only waited twenty-four hours longer, their conduct would surely have been different. The next morning, indeed, the papers of Whaston and elsewhere published, under the signature of J. B. K. Lowenthal, the head of Boston Observatory, a communication which considerably modified the situation, and which, as will be seen, was not very flattering to the two Whaston celebrities.

"Referring," it said, "to statements recently made in the Press by two amateurs of Whaston, we may be allowed to offer a few corrections. And, first, we think it regrettable such statements should have been lightly made without having been previously submitted to the verification of properly qualified men, who, forsooth, are numerous enough and are to be found in all our official observatories.

"It is, no doubt, very glorious to be first in perceiving a celestial body that has the complaisance to traverse the field of a telescope which is turned towards the sky. But a favourable chance of this kind has not the power to transform mere amateurs into professional mathematicians. If, in spite of common sense, problems are tackled which require special competence for their solution, one is liable to commit errors of the kind which it is our duty to correct.

"It is quite true that the bolide every one is talking about has been disturbed in its orbit. But Messrs. Forsyth and Hudelson have acted wrongly in confining themselves to a single observation, and basing on it calculations that are false. Even if we were to take into account only the disturbance manifested on the evening of the 11th of May or the morning of the 12th, we should obtain results differing altogether from theirs. But this is not all. The perturbation of the bolide's movement did not begin or finish between the just-mentioned dates. The first signs of it were visible on the 10th of May, and its action is still at present evident.

"This disturbance, or rather these disturbances, have, on the one hand, brought the bolide nearer to the earth's surface, and, on the other, caused its trajectory to deviate. On the 17th of May, the bolide's distance was about seven or eight kilometres less, and the deviation of its trajectory had attained nearly 0′ 55″.

"This double modification of the previous state of things has not been realized all at once. On the contrary, it is the aggregate amount of a number of minute changes which have not ceased being added to each other since the 10th of the month.

"Until now it has not been possible to discover the cause of the disturbance experienced by the bolide. Nothing in the sky appears capable of producing it. Investigations are continuing on the matter, and unquestionably they will succeed before long.

"But, whatever the cause may be, it is at least premature to announce the fall of this asteroid, and *a fortiori* premature to fix the place and date. Of course, if the unknown cause acting on the bolide continues its influence, the bolide is bound to fall; but so far there is no proof that this influence will continue to be exercised. At present the bolide's speed has necessarily increased, since the orbit is smaller; and, in case the influence should cease acting, there would be no likelihood of the bolide's falling.

"And granting even that the fall will occur, the disturbances noticed each time the meteor passes having been hitherto irregular, and their variations of intensity seeming to follow no law, neither the date nor the place of the fall can be predicted with any precision.

"In fine, we conclude: that the fall of the bolide appears probable, but is not certain. In any case, it is not imminent. We therefore advise people not to excite themselves about an event which remains doubtful of occurrence, and void of practical utility if it does occur. Furthermore, we intend, from now, to keep the public informed every day of what has been discovered and what may be expected."

Whether Mr. Seth Stanfort and Miss Arcadia Walker had cognizance of J. B. K. Lowenthal's communication to the papers we are unable to say. As for the two "amateur astronomers," Mr. Dean Forsyth read it at Saint Louis, and Dr. Sydney Hudelson at New York. To both it was a veritable castigation, which filled them with shame and vexation. However, they were obliged to accept it. Discussion with a savant like Lowenthal was out of the question. They, consequently, returned sheepishly to Whaston, Mr. Dean Forsyth sacrificing his ticket to San Francisco, and Dr. Sydney Hudelson sacrificing his cabin and the price paid for it to Buenos Ayres. On returning to their respective domiciles, they climbed quickly up to their towers, and were compelled to admit that the Boston astronomer was right. When they at last clapped eyes on their vagabond bolide, it was no longer at the place they had assigned it in their inaccurate computations.

Mr. Dean Forsyth and his rival the doctor soon began to suffer for their mistake. Finished the processions that had accompanied them to the station. Gone their popularity. How painful it was to them to be deprived of adulation after tasting its sweets! And now a graver anxiety fell upon them. As Judge Proth had hinted, a third competitor came forward with his claim, announced in the first instance vaguely, then in definite, official language.

This third rival was the whole civilized world, with claims they would be powerless to resist. If they had not been so blinded by their passion and resentment, they might easily have foreseen its intervention. Instead of suing each other in such absurd fashion, they would have bethought themselves that the various governments throughout the world would inevitably be led to take an interest in these wandering milliards, the possession of which might create a most terrible financial crisis. Neither of them had, in fact, anticipated such a contingency, and the announcement of an International Conference on the subject was a thunderbolt to them.

They hastened to make inquiries. The news was correct. Already even the members of the future Conference were designated, which was to meet at Washington, at a date sufficiently distant to allow the delegates of far-away countries to reach the American city conveniently. Yet in order not to be overtaken by events, it was settled by international agreement that, before the arrival of the delegates, some preliminary meetings should be held by the various foreign diplomatists accredited to the American Government. During these preliminary meetings a programme would be drawn up; and, when all the delegates were on the spot, they would be able to begin their labours without delay.

We do not propose to give here the list of the countries represented. As we have just said, the whole of the civilized world had a voice in the matter. No empire, no kingdom, no republic, no principality was left out. All appointed delegates, from Russia and China, represented respectively by Monsieur Ivan Saratoff of Riga and His Excellency Li-Mao-Tchi of Canton, to the Republics of San Marino and Andorra, whose interests would be firmly defended by Messieurs

Beveragi and Ramontcho. All ambitions were permitted; all hopes were lawful, since no one yet knew where the meteor would fall, admitting that it was to fall.

The first preparatory meeting took place on the 25th of May at Washington. It commenced by definitely eliminating the Forsyth-Hudelson claim, dealing with the affair in five minutes. The two rivals, who had come to the city on purpose to defend their rights in person, were refused even a hearing. Their wrath may be imagined as they journeyed back to Whaston. Strange to say, it found no echo outside their own breasts. Not a single paper was found to uphold their cause. Instead of the flattering epithets that were lavished on them a short while before, there was abuse—contempt.

"Why had these two puppets gone to Washington? Suppose they had been the first to draw attention to the bolide! . . . What then? . . . Did such an accident confer any rights upon them? . . . Had they anything to do with its fall? . . . Forsooth, there was no need to discuss such ridiculous pretensions." Such was the tone of the Press at present. *Sic transit gloria mundi!*

After this matter had been got rid of, serious work was proceeded with. Several sittings were devoted to composing the list of sovereign states whose right to take part in the Conference would

THE COMPOSITION OF THE LIST WAS NOT SO EASY AS MIGHT BE IMAGINED

be recognized. Many of them had no regular representative at Washington ; and the decision concerning their collaboration was reserved for the moment when the Conference should enter upon the main subject. The composition of the list was not so easy as might be imagined. For instance, Hungary and Finland demanded direct representation, while Austria and Russia objected. On the other hand, France and Turkey disputed about Tunis, and the Bey's personal intervention in the dispute made it still more complicated. Japan, too, had an argument over Corea. And, in short, most of the nations had analogous questions crop up, so that, after seven sittings, no solution was reached when, on the 1st of June, an unexpected incident occurred to trouble people's minds.

As he had promised, J. B. K. Lowenthal published news about the bolide every day in brief paragraphs which he sent to the newspapers. At first, these communications had nothing in them of particular importance. They simply informed the universe that the meteor's course continued to undergo slight modifications which, in their totality, rendered the fall more and more probable, yet without its being absolutely certain. But the paragraph of the 1st of June was quite different from those that had preceded it. One might almost have thought that the bolide's perturbation was contagious and had power to affect even minds of scientific temper, so disturbed did J. B. K. Lowenthal seem.

"It is not," he said, "without real emotion that we inform the public of the strange phenomena that we have witnessed, facts which tend to sap the bases on which astronomic science reposes, that is to say science in its totality, since human knowledge forms a whole all the parts of which are connected. Yet, however unexplained and inexplicable these phenomena may be, we cannot but admit their irrefragable certitude.

"Our previous communications informed the public that the course of the Whaston bolide had experienced successive and uninterrupted perturbations of which no cause or law had so far been discovered. This fact in itself was sufficiently extraordinary, since the astronomer is able to read the heavens as he would a book, and, as a rule, nothing occurs there that he has not foreseen, or at least that he cannot predict the consequences of. Thus, for example, eclipses, foretold hundreds of years beforehand, occur at the second announced, just as if they obeyed the orders of the perishable being who, time ago, beheld them in the mists of the future, and who, at the moment when his prediction is realized, has been dead for centuries.

"If, however, these perturbations were abnormal, they were not contrary to the data of science, and, if their cause was unknown, we could not accuse anything but the imperfection of our methods of analysis.

"To-day it is not the same. Since the day before yesterday, the course of the bolide has undergone fresh perturbations, and these are in absolute contradiction with our most definite theoretical knowledge. That is to say, we must abandon the hope of ever finding a satisfactory explanation, since the principles hitherto accepted as axioms and on which our calculations are based are no longer applicable.

"The least skilled observer was easily able to remark that the bolide, when passing for the second time during the afternoon of the 30th of May, instead of continuing to draw nearer to the earth, as it had been doing from the 10th of May, had, on the contrary, receded quite perceptibly. On the other hand, the inclination of its orbit, which for twenty days had tended to become more north-east, south-west, had suddenly ceased to accentuate this tendency.

"This unexpected occurrence was already incomprehensible enough. Then, again, yesterday, at the fourth passage of the meteor after sunrise, we were obliged to own that its orbit had again become almost exactly north-south, whilst its distance from the earth had remained without change since the day before.

"Such is the situation at present. Science is powerless to explain facts which would have all the appearances of incoherence, if anything could be incoherent in nature.

"At the time of our first communication we said that the fall, though still uncertain, must be considered as at least probable. Now we do not dare to be so affirmative, and we prefer modestly to confess our ignorance."

If an anarchist had thrown a bomb into the eighth preparatory meeting, he would not have produced an effect comparable to that of this communication signed "J. B. K. Lowenthal." There was a rush for the newspapers that published it with commentaries and an abundance of notes of exclamation. The entire afternoon was spent in nervously exchanging views, to the great detriment of the Conference.

On the following days, things were worse. J. B. K. Lowenthal's communications succeeded each other, with statements more and more surprising. Amidst the marvellously arranged ballet of the stars, the bolide seemed to be dancing a veritable *cancan*, a fantastic hornpipe *sans* rhyme or reason. Now its orbit inclined three degrees in the east, now it frolicked off four degrees in the west. If, at one of its passages, it appeared a little nearer the earth, at the next it had receded several kilometres. It was a Chinese puzzle; nobody knew what to think or say.

This was the case with the International Conference. Dubious as to the utility of their deliberations, the diplomatists put no heart into their confabulations. Yet time was slipping away, and the delegates of all nations were hastening to America and to Washington. Many of them had already arrived; and soon they would be sufficiently numerous to constitute themselves a regular assembly. Were they to find that nothing had been prepared for them to work upon? At length the members of the preliminary committee made an effort, and, in eight further sittings, catalogued the states that were to be admitted, through their deputies, to the labours of the Conference. The number was fixed at fifty-two, namely, twenty-five for Europe, six for Asia, four for Africa, and seventeen for America. They comprised twelve empires, twelve hereditary kingdoms, twenty-two republics, and six principalities. These fifty-two empires, monarchies, republics, and principalities were therefore recognized as being, either by themselves or by their vassals and colonies, sole proprietors of the globe. It was time the preparatory meetings came to this conclusion, for the great majority of the delegates of the fifty-two states admitted to take part in the deliberations were now in Washington, and the remainder were arriving every day.

The International Conference met for the first time on the 10th of June, at two o'clock in the afternoon, under the presidency of the eldest member, who happened to be Monsieur Soliès, professor of oceanography and delegate of the Principality of Monaco. Forthwith, the election of the various officers and the chairman was proceeded with.

Without difficulty the chairmanship was conferred on Mr. Harvey, an eminent jurisconsult representing the United States, the vote being an act of deference and courtesy to the country in which the Conference was held. The vice-chairmanship was not filled without a struggle. It was finally given to Monsieur Saratoff, the delegate of Russia. Next the representatives of England, France, and Japan were chosen as secretaries. These formalities having been settled, the chairman pronounced an amiable speech, which was much applauded, and said that next three sub-committees would be appointed to seek the best means of deliberating at once demographically, financially, and judicially. The vote had just commenced when an apparitor walked up to the chairman and handed him a telegram.

Mr. Harvey read the message, and, as he read, his face expressed an ever-increasing astonishment. However, after a moment's reflection, he shrugged his shoulders disdainfully, a gesture which did not prevent him, after another moment's reflection, from ringing his bell to draw the attention of his colleagues. When silence was obtained, he said :—

'Gentlemen, I think it my duty to inform you

that I have just received this telegram. I cannot doubt but that it is the work of some madman, or else of some one wishing to fool us. I will read you the contents, to which there is no signature.

" 'Mr. Chairman,

" 'I beg to inform the International Conference that the bolide which they have met to discuss about is not *res nullius*, seeing that it is my personal property. The International Conference has no *raison d'être*, and if the members persist in sitting, their deliberations are doomed to failure. It is by my will that the bolide is approaching the earth, by my will that the bolide will fall. To me, therefore, the bolide belongs.' "

"And this telegram is not signed?" queried the English delegate.

"No."

"Then we cannot take it into consideration," declared the representative of Germany.

"That is my opinion," answered the chairman; "and I believe I shall be conforming myself to the unanimous sentiment of my colleagues by placing this document in the archives of the conference . . . Am I right, gentlemen? . . . There is no dissent. . . . Then we will go on with the business."

XIV

In which Widow Thibaut, by thoughtlessly meddling with the most abstruse problems of celestial mechanics, causes grave anxieties to the banker, Robert Lecœur.

SOME folks pretend that, with the progress of morals, sinecures will disappear. We are willing to believe them. But, in any case, at the time of which we are writing one still existed, at least.

This sinecure was the property of Widow Thibaut, whose late husband was a butcher, and who officiated as charwoman in the home of Monsieur Zephyrin Xirdal.

Widow Thibaut's duties consisted in doing the room of this crazy savant. Now, as the furniture of the room was reduced to its simplest expression, the labour of keeping it tidy could hardly be compared to a thirteenth labour of Hercules. As for the rest of the flat, for the most part it was outside of her control. In the second room, indeed, she was absolutely forbidden, whatever the pretext, to touch any of the papers lying around; and it was expressly understood that her broom should limit itself to the small central portion where the floor could be seen.

Widow Thibaut, who was naturally clean and tidy, suffered to see the chaos and disorder that surrounded this little bit of floor, like the sea about an islet, and she itched to proceed to a general spring-clean. Once, being alone in the flat, she had ventured to start on it; but Zephyrin Xirdal, happening to come in upon her unexpectedly, had gone into such a rage, and his good-humoured face had flamed with such fury, that Widow Thibaut had trembled for a week after. Since then she had never risked the least incursion into the territory withdrawn from her authority.

On account of these obstacles to the widow's exercise of her professional talents, she really had not much to do. But none the less, she spent two hours each day in the flat of her "bourgeois"—such was the title she gave to Zephyrin Xirdal; and, out of these two hours, seven quarters were devoted to conversation, or, more strictly speaking, to a monologue in good taste. To her numerous other qualities Widow Thibaut added, truth to tell, an astonishing facility of speech. Some people maintained she was a gossip to a phenomenal degree. But the assertion was malicious. She was fond of talking, nothing more or less.

Not that she went out of her way to find subjects. Generally the distinction of the family that counted her among its members formed the theme of her first discourses. Next, broaching the chapter of her misfortunes, she explained by what unlucky concourse of circumstances a butcher's spouse may be transformed into a servant. It mattered little that this heart-rending story was already known. Widow Thibaut always experienced the same pleasure in relating it. When this subject was exhausted, she would discourse on the various persons she was serving or had served. To the opinions, habits, and peculiarities of these people she compared those of Zephyrin Xirdal, and distributed blame and praise with impartiality.

Her employer, who never replied, was untiringly patient while she said all this. True, since he was lost in his dreams, he did not hear it, which somewhat diminishes the merit that may be considered his due. Anyway, things had gone on so for many years, the one always talking, the other never listening, and both very well satisfied with each other.

On the 30th of May, Widow Thibaut, according to her daily wont, entered Zephyrin Xirdal's flat at nine o'clock in the morning. The savant having departed the day before with his friend Marcel Leroux, his apartments were empty. Widow Thibaut was not much surprised. A long series of similar absences in the past made this one seem quite ordinary. Annoyed only at being deprived of her audience, she did her cleaning as usual. When the bedroom was finished she went into

There, indeed, a surprise awaited her.

the other room, which she called the study. There, indeed, a surprise awaited her.

An unaccustomed object, a sort of dark-looking box, took up a fair portion of that part of the floor which she had the right to sweep. We must explain that Xirdal had always removed it while she cleaned. What did it mean? Resolved not to tolerate this infringement on her prerogative, Widow Thibaut displaced the object with a firm hand and went on quietly with her sweeping. Being rather hard of hearing, she was insensible to the buzzing that came from inside the box; and, as the reflector's bluish light was not very strong, she did not perceive this either. At a certain moment, however, a singular fact forced itself upon her notice. Just when she was passing in front of the metallic reflector, an irresistible push caused her to fall on the floor. In the evening, when she undressed, she was astonished to find a fine black bruise on her right hip. This was all the stranger as she had fallen on her left side. Not chancing again to pass in front of the reflector, she had no further tumble. Consequently she did not for one moment imagine that there was any connection between the displacing of the box and her accident. She thought she had slipped by her own fault.

Widow Thibaut, having a strong sense of duty, did not fail, when she got through with her cleaning, to put back the box in its place. She did her best even—and this justice must be rendered her—to place the box exactly as she had found it. If she did not succeed altogether she must be excused, since it was not on purpose at all that she sent the cylinder of eddying dust in a direction slightly different from that it had previously taken. On the following days she repeated the performance, for, when habits are virtuous and praiseworthy, why should they be changed ?

Yet it must be owned that, becoming familiar, the box progressively lost much of its importance in her eyes, and that she became less and less careful to put it back in its original position after the daily sweep. She never failed, we grant, to drag the box back in front of the window, since Monsieur Zephyrin Xirdal had seen fit to place it there ; but every day the metallic reflector opened its orifice in directions more and more diverse. One day it sent the cylinder of dust a little to the left, another day a little to the right. Widow Thibaut had no bad intention, and did not suspect what cruel anguish her fantastical collaboration was causing to J. B. K. Lowenthal. Once even, by inadvertence, having made the reflector turn on its pivot, she did not see the least inconvenience in its gaping at the ceiling. And, in fact, it was in this position that Zephyrin Xirdal found his machine on returning home in the early afternoon of the 10th of June.

His stay at the seaside had been most agreeable,

and he would perhaps have prolonged it, if, some ten days after his arrival, he had not had the whim to change his linen. Being thus obliged to have recourse to his parcel, he found in it, to his amazement, twenty-seven narrow-necked jars. Zephyrin stared. What was the meaning of these twenty-seven jars? Soon, however, the links in his memory carried him back to his intention of getting an electric pile. After punching himself well as a punishment, he hastened to pack up his twenty-seven jars; and, giving his friend Marcel Leroux the slip, he took the train back to Paris.

It might have happened to him on the way to forget the urgent motive that was taking him home. The thing would have had nothing extraordinary about it. Luckily, an accident that occurred just as he stepped out on to the Saint Lazare platform effectively refreshed his memory. He had packed up his twenty-seven jars so tightly that the parcel burst and the contents crashed and broke on the asphalt with a terrible noise. Two hundred people turned round, thinking it was an anarchist outrage. All they saw was Zephyrin Xirdal contemplating the disaster with a bewildered air.

The breaking of the jars reminded their owner of the reason for which he was back in Paris. So, before mounting to his flat, he called on the druggist and bought twenty-seven other jars, quite new, and on the joiner, who had been vainly waiting for his visit, and had his wheel ready. Laden with these articles, and eager to begin his experiments, he quickly unlocked his door; but stood stock still on the threshold, unable to budge, when he perceived his machine with its reflector turned upwards to the ceiling.

Immediately he recollected everything; and such was the shock he received that his hands let go their burden, which, without any hesitation, dropped to the floor. The wheel was snapped in two, and the twenty-seven jars of the second edition were smashed to bits. This made fifty-four jars broken in less than an hour. If he went on at the same rate, Zephyrin would not be long before he spent the balance of his scandalously good credit account at Monsieur Lecœur's bank.

This remarkable glass-breaker did not so much as perceive the loss. Motionless on his door-mat, he gazed pensively at his machine.

"That's Widow Thibaut all over," he said to himself, as at last he decided to enter.

Raising his eyes, he discovered in the ceiling, and, above the ceiling, in the roof, a small hole situated exactly in the axis of the metallic reflector, in the focus of which the bulb continued to waltz as madly as ever. This hole, which was as big as a pencil, had a bore as clean as if it had been cut with a drilling-machine. A broad smile diffused itself over the face of Zephyrin Xirdal, who was evidently beginning to enjoy himself.

" Well ! . . . Well ! . . . Well ! . . ." he murmured.

However, it was time to intervene. Bending over the machine, he interrupted its working. The buzzing noise ceased, the bluish light went out, and the bulb became almost motionless.

" Well ! . . . Well ! . . . Well ! . . ." repeated Zephyrin, " some nice things must be happening ! "

Impatiently he stripped the bands off the newspapers that lay heaped on the table, and read in succession the communications in which J. B. K. Lowenthal made known to the world the incoherent behaviour of the Whaston bolide. Zephyrin Xirdal literally laughed till he cried. But the subsequent reading of other newspapers made him, on the contrary, frown his forehead. What was this International Conference, the first sitting of which, following on certain preparatory meetings, was announced for that very day ? What need was there to discuss the ownership of the bolide ? Did it not belong to him who was drawing it towards the earth, and but for whom it would have eternally revolved in space ?

However, Zephyrin reflected that no one was aware of his having interfered. It was, therefore, advisable to reveal the fact, so that the International Conference might not lose its time over deliberations which would be necessarily null and void. Kicking the debris of the smashed jars out of his way, he ran to the nearest post office, and sent the telegram which Mr. Harvey read out to the assembled delegates. Afterwards he climbed once more to his rooms; and, having informed himself in a scientific review concerning the variations of the meteor, he fished out his telescope again and made an excellent observation, which served as a basis for fresh calculations.

Towards midnight, having made up his mind what to do, he set his machine going once more, and projected its radiating energy into space with the proper intensity and direction. Then stopping the machine, half an hour later, he went calmly to bed and slept the sleep of the just. The next day, and the day after that, he continued his experiments, and had just interrupted the working of his machine for the third time in the afternoon of this second day, when some one knocked at his door. Opening it, he found himself face to face with the banker, Robert Lecœur.

"Ah! so you're home at last!" cried the banker, entering.

"As you see," answered Zephyrin.

"It's fortunate," continued Monsieur Lecœur. "I don't know how many times I have climbed up your stairs with nothing for my trouble. Where the deuce have you been?"

"I was away," replied Xirdal, blushing slightly in spite of himself.

"Away! . . ." cried the banker indignantly.

" Away ! It's abominable of you to make one so anxious."

Zephyrin looked at his godfather with astonished eyes.

" But, uncle, what difference can it make to you ? " he asked.

" What difference can it make to me ? " repeated the banker. " Don't you know, stupid, that all my fortune depends on you ? "

" I don't understand you," exclaimed Zephyrin, sitting on the table and offering his only chair to his visitor.

" When you came and related your fanciful projects to me," resumed Monsieur Lecœur, " you ultimately convinced me, I confess."

" Egad, I did ! " said Xirdal.

" So I speculated on your luck and went with the bears on 'Change."

" With the bears ? "

" Yes, I sold."

" Sold what ? "

" Gold mines. Don't you see that, if the bolide falls, gold mines will decline, and . . ."

" Will decline ? . . . I understand less and less," interrupted Xirdal. " I don't see what influence my machine can have on the level of a mine."

" Not on the level of a mine," corrected the banker, " but on the value of its shares. That's different."

" Granted," said Zephyrin. " So you've sold

gold mine shares. That's not very serious. That simply proves that you've got some to sell."

"I haven't got one, on the contrary."

"Ah!" exclaimed Xirdal, puzzled. "To sell what one hasn't got is clever. I'm not as cute as that."

"It's what is called speculation on account, my dear Zephyrin," explained Monsieur Lecœur. "When the time comes for handing over the shares, I shall buy some."

"Then what's the advantage? . . . You sell and are obliged to buy; it doesn't strike me as very ingenious."

"That's where you are mistaken. When I buy, mining shares will be cheaper."

"Why should they be cheaper?"

"Because the bolide will throw into the market more gold than the earth at present contains. The value of gold will fall one-half; and mining shares will decline to almost nothing. Do you understand now?"

"Yes," said Xirdal in a tone not over convinced.

"First of all," resumed the banker, "I congratulated myself on having had confidence in you. The disturbances remarked in the bolide's course, and its fall being announced as certain, produced a decline of twenty-five per cent in mining values. Being convinced that the decline would continue, I speculated largely."

"You mean . . ."

"That I sold a still greater number of mining shares."

"Still without having any to sell?"

"Of course. . . . You may fancy my anxiety when I found that you had vanished, that the bolide had ceased falling and was wandering about in the four quarters of the heavens. The result is that mining shares have gone up, and I have lost enormous sums. What am I to think of it all?"

Zephyrin Xirdal looked at his godfather with curiosity. He had never seen this man of cold manners a prey to such emotion.

"I haven't very well comprehended all you have told me," he said at length. "Such things are not in my line. What I do think I understand, however, is that you would like the bolide to fall. Well! you can make your mind easy. The bolide shall fall."

"You guarantee it."

"Yes."

"Positively?"

"Positively. But have you bought my piece of land?"

"Of course," replied Monsieur Lecœur. "I have the deed of sale in my pocket."

"Then everything is all right," approved Zephyrin. "I can even announce to you that my experiment will finish on the fifth of July. On that day I shall quit Paris, and shall go to meet the bolide."

"Which will fall?"

"Which will fall."

"I will start with you!" cried the banker gleefully.

"If you like!" said Zephyrin.

Whether it was the consciousness of his responsibility to Monsieur Robert Lecœur, or merely his passion for science and the interest of his present attempt, Zephyrin Xirdal managed to go through with the experiment without any further fit of absent-mindedness; and the mysterious machine buzzed and hummed until the 5th of July a little over fourteen times each twenty-four hours. From time to time Zephyrin effected an astronomic observation of the meteor, and was able to ascertain that everything was turning out according to his anticipations. During the morning of the 5th of July, he looked through his telescope for the purpose of a last verification.

"It's all right now," he said, as he left the instrument. "We can let things slide at present."

At once he began preparing his luggage. First he cleverly packed up his machine and telescope, putting in the parcel a few spare bulbs, and protecting everything breakable by padded cases. Then he bethought himself of his personal necessaries. A serious difficulty met him here. He had never had a travelling trunk, and he wondered in what he was to carry these articles. After a good deal of reflection, he remembered that he had a portmanteau; and this he ultimately found in a dark closet under a heap of rubbish. It was minus straps and had but little of its pristine elegance. Zephyrin opened it, such as it was, and stood musingly gazing at the inside. What should he deposit there?

"Nothing but what is strictly requisite," he said to himself. "So I must make a selection."

In virtue of this decision, he began by his footgear; and, his mind running on what was to come next, he placed side by side in a corner of the portmanteau one buttoned boot, one laced boot, and one slipper. Later he awoke to the inconvenience of his choice. For the moment it did not strike him. Fatigued by the efforts of this novel occupation, he paused and wiped his forehead; and, not being able to decide what he should choose next, he next plunged his hands into the linen and clothes that lay in his wardrobe and chest of drawers, and, taking what was uppermost, thrust it into the portmanteau. When this summary operation was accomplished, he tied some string round the portmanteau in knots so intricate that they would subsequently want a day's work to undo.

It remained for him to get to the station with his *impedimenta*. In spite of his walking powers, Zephyrin could not hope to go on foot with his machine, telescope, and other luggage under his arm. He felt embarrassed. Probably he would have recollected, by dint of cudgelling his brains, that cabs were to be had in Paris. Happily this intellectual labour was spared him. Monsieur Robert Lecœur appeared at the door.

"Well! are you ready, Zephyrin?" he asked.

"I was waiting for you," answered Xirdal ingenuously; he had quite forgotten that his godfather was to start with him.

"Let's be off, then," said the banker. "What luggage have you got?"

"Three things: my machine, my telescope, and my portmanteau."

"Give me one, and take the two others yourself. My carriage is down below."

"What a good idea!" admired Zephyrin Xirdal, closing his door behind him.

XV

In which J. B. K. Lowenthal designates the winner of the prize.

SINCE they had committed the error so sharply criticized by J. B. K. Lowenthal—their first mishap, soon followed by the humiliating refusal of the International Conference to admit their claim—the two Whaston astronomers had looked on life somewhat sourly. It was hard for them, who had tasted of the sweets of fame, to be forgotten, relegated to the ranks of ordinary citizens. In conversations with their few remaining adherents, they inveighed violently against the blindness of the mob, and defended their cause with manifold arguments.

If they had made a mistake, was it just to reproach them with it? Had not their critic, J. B. K. Lowenthal himself, been mistaken also, and had he not been finally obliged to own his inability to explain what was taking place? What other conclusion was possible save that their bolide was something exceptional and abnormal? Under such circumstances, was not an error most natural and most excusable?

"Certainly!" answered the few faithful ones.

As for the International Conference, could anything more iniquitous be imagined than its denial of justice? That it should take precautions for the safeguarding of the world's finances was quite right and proper! But how could its members deny the claims of him who had discovered the meteor? Would not the bolide have continued to be unknown, and, if its fall were to occur, would it have been predicted without the aid of the man who had drawn the world's attention first to the bolide?

"And this discoverer is I!" affirmed Mr. Dean Forsyth with still the same energy.

"I," on his side, affirmed Dr. Sydney Hudelson just as energetically.

"Certainly!" approved the faithful few.

Though the consolations of these few were something, they did not replace the lost admiration of the crowd. However, neither of the rivals showed any signs of diminishing their vain pretensions, or of returning to a more reasonable state of mind with regard to each other. And the unfortunate couple, Francis and Jenny, had still to suffer from their enmity. Francis did not abandon the house in Elizabeth Street, but he never spoke now to his uncle; and, as Mitz no longer gave free rein to her eloquence, the house was as dull as a cloister. At Dr. Hudelson's life was scarcely more cheerful. Loo refused to say a word to her father, notwithstanding his suppliant glances. Jenny was more often than not in tears, in spite of her mother's exhortations. Mrs. Hudelson herself sighed and hoped that time would remedy this situation, which was as ridiculous as it was detestable. No doubt she was right; yet one must confess that time was in no hurry, on this occasion, to improve the relations of the two unhappy families.

Although Mr. Dean Forsyth and Dr. Hudelson were conscious of the reprobation with which they were regarded, it did not inflict upon them the grief they would have felt under other circumstances. Their fixed idea steeled them against public and private opinion. The bolide filled their hearts and minds; to it went out all their aspirations. How eagerly they perused the daily letters of J. B. K. Lowenthal and the accounts of the sittings of the International Conference! Their common enemies were in the Conference, and they were united in hatred of everything and every one belonging to it. Keen was their satisfaction on learning what difficulties cropped up at the preparatory meetings; and keener when they saw how doubtful was the prospect of there being any agreement reached, and how manifest was the strain.

In its second sitting the Conference had already given the impression that it would hardly succeed in settling anything. Notwithstanding the studies carried out by the various sub-committees, the tendency to dissent increased. The first definite proposal made was that the bolide should become the property of the country on whose territory it should fall. This was equivalent to making the matter a lottery in which there would be one prize only, and a big one! The proposal, which was put forward by Russia, and seconded by Great Britain and China, was received with a good deal of hesitancy. The sitting was suspended. There were palavers and intriguing behind the scenes. Finally, in order to gain time, a motion of adjournment, proposed by Switzerland, was voted by the Conference. This meant that the one prize scheme would be adopted only if it were impossible to agree in an equitable division all round.

But how, in such a case, decide what was equitable and what was not? The problem was a delicate one. Numerous sittings were devoted to the question, without any solution being arrived at; and some of the sittings were so noisy that Mr. Harvey was compelled to leave the chair. Even this way of calming the members might not always serve. The irritation was growing; and it seemed likely that before long the sittings would become so tumultuous as to need the employment of force for the restoration of order, which would be prejudicial to the dignity of the sovereign states represented at the Conference.

Calmness, indeed, was hardly to be expected,

when the daily communications made by J. B. K. Lowenthal to the Press announced the fall of the bolide as being more and more probable. After about ten letters relating the mad antics of the meteor, and betraying the astronomer's annoyance, there was a change. In the night of the 11th to the 12th of July, the astronomer had recovered his peace of mind on discovering that the bolide, ceasing its frolic, was being again acted on by a regular and constant power, which, although unknown, was not contrary to reason. The cause of the aberration he meant to investigate later. For the moment he contented himself with informing the world of this return to a normal condition, and of the fresh diminution of the meteor's distance from the earth, according to a progression so far undetermined. The orbit, at the same time, had begun once more to incline towards the north-east south-west; and J. B. K. Lowenthal at present regarded the bolide's fall as being almost certain.

What an incentive for the Conference to hasten the conclusion of its deliberations!

In his last communications between the 5th and 14th of July, the learned head of the Boston Observatory was bolder still in his statements. He hinted more plainly every day that he would soon have an important announcement to make.

It happened that on the 14th of July the International Conference came to a dead-lock. Every possible combination had been discussed and rejected in turn. The delegates looked at each other in embarrassment. How were they to resume the consideration of a question which had been already threshed out to no purpose?

In the first sittings the proposal to divide the meteor's milliards in proportion to the superficial area of the various countries had been voted down, in spite of its equitableness. Although the countries of large area might be supposed to have greater needs, and although, as a matter of fact, they sacrificed their more numerous chances in consenting to a division, no account was made of their forbearance by other countries whose population was dense and whose area was relatively small.

These latter wished the distribution to be in proportion to the number of inhabitants in each territory. This system, which also was not altogether unjust, since it respected the equal rights of individuals, was opposed by Russia, Brazil, the Argentine Republic, and several other countries sparsely inhabited. Mr. Harvey sided with the opposition, and, as the voting was equal without him, enabled the non-contents to have their way by twenty against nineteen.

Governments, whose finances were indicative of large annual deficits, then suggested it would be equitable to divide the gold fallen from the sky in such a manner that the lot of all the inhabitants of the earth should be equalized. Objection was immediately offered on the score that this system, of a socialistic character, would constitute a premium on idleness, and would involve a distribution so complicated as to be practically infeasible. None the less, certain speakers brought forward amendments tending to notice being taken of the three factors: area, population, wealth, and to each of the factors being assigned a co-efficient conforming to equity.

Equity! The word was in every one's mouth. Whether it was in every one's heart is less sure; which was probably why these solutions were rejected like the others, each and all of the delegates hoping for some particular advantage.

In face of the dead-lock, Russia and China deemed the movement opportune to revive the proposal first voted down by its adjournment, and to try to get it adopted with some little modification. These two states, therefore, suggested that the milliards should be handed over to one of the nations, to be chosen by lot, the winner to pay the losing countries an indemnity calculated at a thousand francs for each citizen.

Perhaps, through lassitude, this compromise would have been accepted on the evening of the 14th of July, if the Republic of Andorra had not objected. Its representative, Monsieur Ramontcho, began an interminable speech that might have been going on perhaps now if the chairman, seeing that every seat was vacant, had not adjourned the discussion till the morrow.

Although the Republic of Andorra, whose preferences were for a distribution based on the number of inhabitants, believed it was pursuing a good policy in thwarting the immediate acceptance of Russia's proposal, it made a grievous mistake. Whereas the proposal assured the Republic, in any case, advantages that were appreciable, there was now a great probability of its receiving nothing at all, a result not foreseen by Monsieur Ramontcho, who would have done better to hold his tongue.

During the morning of the 15th of July, something was going to happen which would discredit the International Conference and definitely compromise its chances of success. If it had been possible, as long as no one knew where the bolide would fall, to discuss every conceivable manner of distributing the milliards, such discussion was useless when the place of the fall was known. At any rate, no country whose territory should receive the bolide would consent to share its booty voluntarily. And, as a matter of fact, after the 14th of July, there was one delegate, Monsieur de Schnack, the representative of Greenland, who deserted the sittings of the Conference. For in the papers of the 15th this is what J. B. K. Lowenthal published :

" During the last ten days we have several

times spoken of important changes that were occurring in the meteor's course. To-day we are able to speak with greater precision, since the length of our observations has allowed us to convince ourselves of the permanent character of these changes, and to determine what will result from them.

"Since the 5th of July, the power previously acting on the meteor has not made itself felt. From that date forward there has been no further deviation in the bolide's orbit, and the bolide has approached the earth only by reason of the earth's ordinary attraction overcoming its centrifugal velocity. To-day its distance is about fifty kilometres.

"If the unknown influence acting on the bolide had ceased a few days earlier, the bolide, by virtue of its centrifugal force, might have escaped the earth's attraction sufficiently to enable it to return almost to its original distance. At present this cannot be. The meteor's speed, reduced by friction in the denser strata of the atmosphere, is only just enough to keep it in its trajectory. And, since the cause of its diminished speed is a permanent one, we may hold it for certain now that the bolide will fall.

"Moreover, as the air's resistance is a factor in the problem which is known, we are able to trace the curve of the meteor's fall. Reservation made of unexpected complications, which our preceding experience forbids us to consider impossible, we may here state that:

"(1) The bolide will fall.

"(2) It will fall between two and nine o'clock in the morning of the 19th of August.

"(3) It will fall within a radius of ten kilometres round the town of Upernivik, the capital of Greenland."

If the banker, Robert Lecœur, read this communication, he must have been pleased. Scarcely had the news been published when there was a slump in mining shares in the markets of every continent, reducing them to about a fifth merely of their previous value.

XVI

In which a number of sightseers profit by the opportunity to go to Greenland and be present at the fall of the extraordinary meteor.

On the 27th of July, in the morning, a numerous crowd was watching the steamer *Mozik*, which was about to leave Charleston, the great port of South Carolina. So many were the excursionists wishing to go to Greenland, that, for some days past, not a cabin had been available on board this vessel of fifteen hundred tons, although it was not the only one freighted and bound to the same place. A number of other steamers belonging to different countries were preparing to sail up the Atlantic as far as Davis Strait and Baffin Bay, beyond the limits of the Arctic Polar Circle.

This affluence of passengers was not surprising, considering the excitement of people's minds since J. B. K. Lowenthal's communication to the Press. The learned astronomer could not have calculated wrongly. After trouncing Messrs. Forsyth and Hudelson for their mistakes, he would scarcely have ventured to expose himself to a like castigation. Indeed, under the circumstances, it would have been inexcusable on his part to speak without certitude.

Consequently his conclusions must be admitted; and the bolide would fall undoubtedly, not in unapproachable polar regions or in the depths of the sea, whence no human hand could rescue it, but really and truly on the territory of Greenland. It was this vast region, once dependent upon Denmark, but to which independence had been generously granted a few years before the meteor's appearance, that fortune was about to favour in preference to all the other countries of the universe.

The territory, indeed, was a huge one, so large that one was puzzled to decide whether it was a continent or an island. The golden sphere might have fallen in a part far from the shore, some hundreds of leagues inland, and, in such a case, the difficulty of reaching it would have been enormous. Of course, the difficulty would have been dealt with; both arctic cold and snow-storm would have been braved; and the pole itself would have been attained, if necessary, in pursuit of the milliards. It was extremely lucky no one would be obliged to make such efforts, and that the place of the fall had been indicated so exactly. Greenland was far enough for any one, without emulating the exploits of Parry, Nansen, and other explorers of hyperborean latitudes.

If the reader could have embarked on the

Mozik, he would have seen amongst the many other passengers, with a fair sprinkling of women, five persons whose faces he would have immediately recognized. Nor would he have been astonished at the presence of at least four of them. One was Mr. Dean Forsyth, who, in company with Omicron, was navigating far from Elizabeth Street; a third was Dr. Sydney Hudelson, who had left his tower in Morris Street. As soon as they had cognizance of these excursions to Greenland, the two rivals did not hesitate to take a return ticket and start. In fact, in case of need, they would each have chartered a vessel of their own to Upernivik. Evidently they were aware that they could not seize the block of gold, appropriate it, and bring it back to Whaston; but they intended to be on the spot at the moment it fell. Who could tell if the Government of Greenland would not, after all, in taking possession of the bolide, assign to them a portion of these milliards fallen from the sky? . . .

Naturally, on board the *Mozik*, Mr. Forsyth and the doctor had been careful to select cabins that were not side by side. During the voyage, as at Whaston, they would have no connection with each other. Mrs. Hudelson had not attempted to stop her husband from going, any more than Mitz had attempted to dissuade her master from the journey. However, the doctor had been induced by Jenny's entreaties and the consciousness of his own harshness towards her to let his elder daughter go with him. Jenny's reason for wishing to accompany her father was her expectation of Francis' being one of his uncle's party. And she was right. Francis said to himself that, since the marriage was temporarily deferred, he would do more wisely to make the excursion and to watch for an opportunity of modifying the deplorable situation that existed between the two rivals. And now that Jenny was going, he hoped, as she did, that they would be able to enjoy some little of each other's society.

In his inmost heart Francis trusted that J. B. K. Lowenthal had been guilty of some trifling error and that the bolide would tumble into the depths of the Arctic Ocean. If this happened, no doubt a reconciliation could be brought about between his uncle and the doctor. There was one person that such a dénouement would disappoint, to wit, Monsieur Ewald de Schnack, Greenland's representative at the International Conference, who was also among the passengers on board the *Mozik*. His country was about to become the richest in the world. To accommodate so many milliards, the Government's coffers would not be either large or numerous enough.

Happy nation, in which henceforth there would be no tax, and poverty would no longer exist! Owing to the thrift of the Scandinavian race, this huge mass of gold would be no doubt spent only with extreme prudence. So there was reason to hope the money market would not suffer too much from the shower of gold that Jupiter was pouring into Danaë's lap.

Monsieur de Schnack was the hero on board. Mr. Dean Forsyth and Dr. Hudelson were ignored in the presence of Greenland's delegate, and, whenever they met him, they burned alike in resentment towards the representative of a State that took from them not only their material, but their moral, advantages in connection with the bolide.

The voyage from Charleston to the capital of Greenland was to take about a fortnight, the distance being three thousand three hundred miles. A call was to be made at Boston for the purpose of coaling. As for provisions, enough were carried to last several months, by this and every other vessel, since the existence of so many visitors to Upernivik could hardly else have been assured.

At first the *Mozik* steamed north, hugging the eastern coast of the United States. But the day after the departure, when Cape Hatteras, the extreme point of North Carolina, had been passed, the vessel put out to sea. In the month of July, the sky is generally fine in these parts of the Atlantic; and, as long as the wind blew from the west, the sea remained calm. At times, unfortunately, there was a sharp breeze from the open, and then the vessel's pitching and rolling produced their usual effects.

If Monsieur de Schnack was hardened against sea-sickness by the prospect of his country's milliards, Mr. Forsyth and Dr. Hudelson were not. It was their first voyage, and they paid large tribute to Neptune. Yet not for a single instant did they regret having embarked on this adventure. We need scarcely say that their indisposition was taken advantage of by Francis and Jenny. Neither of them was sea-sick; and so they both enjoyed nice long chats while the two astronomers were moaning and groaning under the treacherous attacks of Amphitrite. When they quitted each other, it was to go and offer aid to the two invalids; and, slily, they managed that it should be generally Francis who consoled Dr. Hudelson, and Jenny who consoled Mr. Dean Forsyth.

When the sea's swell was less perceptible, the two lovers led the two astronomers out of their cabins on to the spar-deck, and seated them each on a cane-bottomed chair, contriving to diminish the distance between the two chairs progressively.

"How do you feel?" asked Jenny, as she covered up Mr. Forsyth's legs.

"Very poorly," sighed the invalid, hardly conscious of who it was that addressed him.

And having arranged the doctor's cushions, Francis asked him how he was as affably as if

NEITHER OF THEM WAS SEA-SICK

Jenny's father had never forbidden him to think of marrying Jenny.

The two rivals stayed there some hours, only vaguely realizing how near they were to each other. To restore them to animation it needed that Monsieur de Schnack should pass by, with well-assured gait, like an old jack-tar mocking at the waves, and with the head of a man who dreamed only of gold and saw everything in gold. A sombre flash then lit up the eyes of the two invalids, who found strength to launch a muttered invective.

"The robber!" said Mr. Forsyth.

"The thief!" echoed Dr. Hudelson.

Monsieur de Schnack gave no attention. He did not even condescend to remark their presence on board. He went disdainfully to and fro with the coolness of a man about to find in his country more than enough money to pay off the national debt of every people in the world.

Meanwhile the voyage continued, on the whole, under favourable auspices. Presumably, other ships, starting from various ports, were sailing northwards towards Davis Strait, and more were crossing with like intent from the other side of the Atlantic. The *Mozik* passed by New York without calling, and, steaming north-east, pursued her way towards Boston. On the morning of the 30th of July she cast anchor outside the capital of the State of Massachusetts. One day would be sufficient to fill her coal bunkers up to the top—the largest supply possible being needed to last to Greenland and back.

Although the voyage had not been a rough one so far, most of the passengers had suffered from sea-sickness, and five or six preferred to go no farther than Boston, and disembarked. Not one of them was Mr. Dean Forsyth or Dr. Hudelson. These gentlemen meant to go on, and, if the journey were to cost them their life, they would breathe their last sigh in view of the meteor.

The landing of the few less persevering travellers left some cabins free on board the *Mozik;* these were soon provided with amateurs desirous of starting from Boston. Among the latter might have been remarked a gentleman of fine bearing, who had come to the ship's side, immediately after the arrival in the harbour, to ask if there were a vacant cabin. This gentleman was no other than Mr. Seth Stanfort. After the divorce, Mr. Stanfort had returned to Boston. Still hankering after fresh travels, and being obliged to acknowledge, from J. B. K. Lowenthal's first letter, the uselessness of his going to Japan, he had visited during the last two months the chief towns in Canada: Quebec, Toronto, Montreal, Ottawa. Was he trying to forget his divorced wife? There seemed to be no necessity. The two spouses had pleased each other to begin with; then they ceased to please each other. A

To restore them to animation, it needed that Monsieur de Schnack should pass by

divorce as original as their marriage had separated them from each other. That was the sum of the matter. No doubt they would not meet again, or, if they met, would not recognize each other.

Mr. Seth Stanfort had just arrived at Toronto when he learnt the news published by J. B. K. Lowenthal concerning the bolide's fall in Greenland. Even if it had been announced to take place some thousands of leagues farther in the most remote regions of Asia or Africa, he would, nevertheless, have done his utmost to go thither. Not that he was particularly interested in this meteoric phenomenon; but the opportunity of witnessing a spectacle at which there would be comparatively few persons, of beholding what millions of human beings would not behold, was something to tempt an adventurous gentleman fond of trotting about, whose fortune permitted him to indulge in the most fantastic travels. Now on this occasion he was not required to proceed to the Antipodes. The stage on which was to be played this astronomic pantomime was within easy distance of Canada.

Mr. Seth Stanfort, therefore, took the first train to Quebec; then the first for Boston, travelling through the plains of the Dominion and New England. Forty-eight hours after he had embarked, the *Mozik*, without losing sight of land, passed off Portsmouth, then off Portland, within hearing of the signalling stations. Perhaps these were able to give news about the bolide, which could be perceived at present with the naked eye when the sky was clear.

The semaphores remained mute, and that of Halifax was no more communicative when the steamer came opposite this great port of New Scotland. How sorry the passengers were that the Bay of Fundy, between New Scotland and New Brunswick, offered no issue either to the east or to the north! In that case they would not have had to put up with the swell which troubled them as far as the island of Cape Breton. The victims to sea-sickness were numerous, among them again being, in spite of Francis's and Jenny's care, Mr. Forsyth and Dr. Hudelson.

The captain of the *Mozik* had pity on his suffering guests. He cruised through the Gulf of St. Lawrence and returned to the high seas through the Strait of Belle Isle, under the lee of Newfoundland. Thence he proceeded towards the western coast of Greenland, crossing Davis Strait in the widest part. In this way the voyage was rendered easier.

Cape Comfort was sighted in the morning of the 7th of August. The territory of Greenland ends rather more in the east, at Cape Farewell, against which dash the waves of the Northern Atlantic. And with what fury know only too well the courageous fishers of Newfoundland and Iceland. Happily there was no need to skirt the eastern coast of Greenland, which is almost unapproachable and offers no refuge to vessels, since it is washed by the open sea's swell. On the other hand, sheltered spots are not wanting in Davis Strait. Either in the depths of the fiords or behind the islets, it is easy to take refuge; and, except when the wind blows direct from the south, navigation is practicable under favourable conditions. The voyage, therefore, continued without the passengers' having much to complain of.

The part of the coast of Greenland between Cape Farewell and Disko Island is for the most part bordered by cliffs of primitive rock, fairly lofty, which check winds coming from the sea. Even during the winter period this shore is less blocked by ice, which is brought from the northern ocean by polar currents.

At length the *Mozik* arrived in Gilbert Bay, and some hours later touched at Goodhaab, where the ship's cook was able to procure fresh fish in large quantities, this article of diet being, in fact, a staple food of the Greenlanders. From here the vessel proceeded past the ports of Holsteinborg and Christianshaab. These places are so enclosed within their rocky walls—the second right back in Disko Bay—that their existence can hardly be suspected by any one out at sea. They afford retreat to the numerous fishers that frequent Davis Strait in search of whales, narvals, walruses, and seals, and venture sometimes to the farthest limits of Baffin Bay.

Disko Island, which the steamer reached early on the 9th of August, is the most important of all the small isles that cluster along the coast of Greenland. Its chief town, Goodhaven, is built on the northern coast, which, like the rest of the island, is of basaltic formation. The houses are not, however, of stone, but of wood, with their rough-hewn beam walls rendered impervious to air by a thick coating of tar. Francis Gordon and Seth Stanfort, being less preoccupied by the meteor than the rest of the passengers, were struck by the appearance of this dark-looking mass of buildings, whose red-painted roofs and windows contrasted agreeably with the more sombre portions. What must life be here during winter? They would have been much astonished to learn that it was almost the same as in Stockholm or Copenhagen. Certain houses, though scantily furnished, are not without comfort. They have a drawing-room, dining-room, and library even; for high society, if we may use the term, being Danish in origin, is not without culture. The executive is represented by a delegate of the Government, whose seat is at Upernivik.

In the harbour of this last town, after leaving the island of Disko behind her, the *Mozik* cast anchor on the 10th of August about six o'clock in the evening.

XVII

In which a passenger of the "Mozik" meets with a passenger of the "Oregon," and the marvellous bolide at last meets with the terrestrial globe.

FOR this snow-covered country White Land would be a more correct appellation than Greenland. Maybe, it was so-called ironically by its godfather, Eric the Red, a tenth-century sailor, who, most likely, was no redder than the land he named is green. Perhaps this Scandinavian was hoping to induce his fellow-countrymen to come and colonize this green (!) hyperborean region. If so, he did not succeed very well. Colonists have not allowed themselves to be tempted by the title; and at present, even including natives, the population of Greenland is scarcely more than ten thousand.

One must admit that a bolide worth so many milliards might have chosen a country better fitted than this one to receive it. And such a reflection must have occurred to the mind of more than one passenger led by curiosity to Upernivik. Would it not have been quite as easy for the bolide to fall a few hundred leagues farther south, on the broad plains of the Dominion or the Union, where finding it would have been so much more convenient? Now it was a most impracticable sort of country which was about to be the scene of this memorable event.

To tell the truth, there were precedents. Bolides had already fallen in Greenland. In Disko Island, Nordenskiold found three blocks of iron, each weighing twenty-four tons, which were probably meteorites. These at present figure in the Stockholm Museum.

Fortunately, if J. B. K. Lowenthal had not made a mistake, the bolide was to fall in a region fairly easy of access, and during the month of August, which raised the temperature above freezing-point. At this season of the year, the ground can here and there justify the ironical appellation of Greenland conferred on it. In the gardens grow some few vegetables and grasses, whereas farther inland the botanist finds only mosses and lichens. On the coast-line, pastures appear after the melting of the ice, which pastures allow of small quantities of cattle being kept. Forsooth, neither oxen nor cows are to be counted by hundreds; but poultry and goats may be met with, of a hardy kind, not to speak of reindeer and the numerous dog population. Of course, after two or three months of milder weather, the winter returns with its long nights, its bleak winds from the polar regions, and its dreadful blizzards. Over the carapace covering the ground a sort of grey dust flies and hovers, called ice dust; it is the cryokonite full of microscopic plants, the first specimens of which were collected by Nordenskiold.

Since the meteor was not to descend in the interior of Greenland, there was, in any case, room for doubt as to that country's finally possessing it. Upernivik is not only on the seashore; it is on an island, amidst a whole series of other isles; and, having a circumference of less than ten miles, it was a narrow target for the aerial ball to hit. If the ball missed the shore by ever so little, it would tumble into the waters of Baffin Bay. And the sea is deep in these parts, between one and two thousand yards. To fish up a mass of nearly nine hundred thousand tons would be an impossible task. Monsieur de Schnack was gravely preoccupied; and, having made acquaintance with Seth Stanfort on the voyage, he had spoken to him more than once of this contingency. But there was nothing to be done except to wait and see how far J. B. K. Lowenthal's predictions would be verified.

Save Francis and Jenny, who, as we have said, would have only been too pleased for the bolide to tumble into the sea, the other passengers of the *Mozik* and of the rest of the ships that lay anchored in front of Upernivik, were also preoccupied. Having made the voyage, they wanted to have some reward for their trouble. There was, at least, one thing in their favour, the absence of darkness. For eighty days, that is to say, forty days before the summer solstice and forty days after, in this latitude, the sun is continually above the horizon. They would, therefore, have the greatest chance of seeing whatever happened if, in conformity with J. B. K. Lowenthal's declarations, the meteor fell anywhere near the station.

On the day following their arrival a crowd of people were to be found inquisitively examining the wooden houses of Upernivik, the principal building being adorned with the white flag and red cross of the country. Never had the inhabitants of Greenland had so many visitors at once come to inspect their buildings.

Curious types, these Greenlanders appeared to be, especially on the western coast. Short or medium-sized, thick-set, stalwart, with little legs, slender hands and wrists, sallow-skinned, their faces broad and flat, noses of diminutive proportions, eyes brown and slightly drawn together, hair black and coarse, falling about their cheeks, they had a certain resemblance to their seals, possessing the latter's mild physiognomy, and also the comfortable coating of fat protecting them against the cold. Both sexes wore the same sort of dress: boots, trousers, "amaout" or hood. However, the members of the fair sex,

A crowd of people were to be found inquisitively examining the wooden houses of Upernivik

graceful and merry when young, wore their hair like a helmet, and decked themselves out in modern stuffs and parti-coloured ribbons. The former fashion of tattooing the skin has now disappeared from among these people; but they have preserved their taste for singing and dancing, which are their only amusements. Their drink is water; their food the flesh of seals and certain edible dogs, together with fish and berries of seaweed. Not a very gay life for them.

The advent of so many strangers in the island of Upernivik greatly surprised the few hundred natives; and, when they learnt the cause that brought them, the surprise did not diminish. Not that they were ignorant of the value of gold; but they knew that the windfall would be of no profit to themselves. If these milliards fell on their land, the gold would not go into their pockets, in spite of their having pockets to fill. They would go into the State's coffers, whence, according to custom, no one would see them come out again. Yet they could not altogether fail to be interested. Perhaps some benefit might accrue to them—these poor citizens of Greenland.

Meanwhile, the hour for the decisive event was drawing very near. If other steamers should arrive, the port of Upernivik would be not large enough to hold them. On the other hand, those that were there could not hope to prolong their stay much over the date fixed. With September would begin winter, and ice; and Baffin Bay would become impracticable. They would have to sail southwards, leaving behind them Cape Farewell, under penalty of being caught by the floes and blocked in for seven or eight months.

While waiting, the intrepid tourists made long excursions about the island. Its rocky, flat surface, with just a few low hills in the middle portions, was easy for walking on. Here and there were plains where, above a carpet of moss and yellowish-looking grass, grew shrubs that would never develop into trees, a few dwarf birches that still are to be found beyond the seventy-second degree of latitude. The sky was generally misty, and, more often than not, was swept by big clouds under the blast of east winds. The temperature never rose higher than fifty degrees Fahrenheit. Consequently, the tourists were glad to return to their vessels in search of comforts that they could hardly have obtained in the village, and food that was procurable neither at Godhaven nor at any other station on the coast.

Five days had thus gone by since the *Mozik* had cast anchor, when, on the morning of the 16th of August, a last vessel was signalled off Upernivik. She was a steamer that was threading her way through the isles and islets of the Archipelago, in order to get into convenient anchorage. At her masthead fluttered the flag of the United States. It was evident that she was bringing a fresh crowd of sight-seers, late-comers, but yet in time, since the globe of gold was still circling up in the air. About eleven in the morning, the *Oregon*, for this was the steamer's name, came alongside, having previously disembarked one of the passengers, who was apparently in a hurry, in one of the small boats that she carried on board.

This passenger belonged to the Boston Observatory astronomers, a Mr. Wharf, who at once proceeded to the residence of the Government's representative in Upernivik. The latter went and informed Monsieur de Schnack, and he forthwith came to speak to the astronomer. Every one was in a fever of anxiety. Was the bolide, perchance, going, after all, to take French leave and depart to other regions, as Francis Gordon had hoped it would ? Soon the tourists were reassured. J. B. K. Lowenthal's calculations were correct; and, if Mr. Wharf had undertaken this long journey, it was simply to be present at the bolide's fall, in lieu of his superior.

The 16th of August. In thrice twenty-four hours the meteor would rest on Greenland's soil.

"Unless it goes to the bottom of the sea," murmured Francis and Jenny.

Three days wasn't much, and yet it was long waiting in a place where pleasures were few. The visitors were bored, and yawned enough to break their jaws. However, one of them seemed to be enjoying himself fairly well, to wit, Mr. Seth Stanfort. Being such an inveterate globe-trotter, he was accustomed to find himself in all sorts of places and to keep himself company. Perhaps to reward him for his good-humour, or perhaps to prove once more the injustice of fortune, fate chose him alone, of all that were there, for an encounter that was unexpected. He was walking along the beach to watch the *Oregon* land her passengers, when he was checked by the sight of a lady who had just got off the boat. Mistrusting his eyes, Seth Stanfort went forward to meet the lady, and said in a tone expressive of astonishment without displeasure:

"Miss Arcadia Walker, if I am not mistaken."

"Ah! Mr. Stanfort!" replied the lady.

"I little thought, Miss Arcadia, to see you on this far-away island."

"And I little thought to see you, Mr. Stanfort."

"Well! how are you, Miss Arcadia?"

"Capital! Mr. Stanfort . . . and you?"

"Very well indeed!"

Thereupon they began to chat like two old acquaintances that had just come together by the greatest chance.

"So it has not yet fallen?" exclaimed Miss Walker, raising her hand towards the sky.

"No, it is still in the air; but it will fall soon."

"I shall be there to witness it!" said the lady, with a lively satisfaction.

"And I too," replied Mr. Seth Stanfort.

Decidedly these were two very distinguished persons, two people of the world, not to say two old friends, whom a like feeling of curiosity had caused to find each other again on this Upernivik beach.

Why, after all, should it have been otherwise? Miss Arcadia Walker, indeed, had not discovered her ideal in Seth Stanfort; but perhaps such an ideal did not exist, since she had discovered him nowhere else. Never had she been smitten, as lovers in novels are smitten, with that irresistible bolt of Cupid known as love at first sight; and, in default of it, never had her heart either been conquered by some service sufficiently striking to make her yield. After an honest experiment, she had concluded marriage did not suit her any more than it suited Mr. Seth Stanfort; but, whilst she felt a certain liking only for a man who had been delicate enough to give up being her husband, he preserved, of his ex-wife, the memory of an intelligent, original woman, who had become absolutely perfect as soon as she ceased to be his spouse. They had separated without reproach or recrimination. Mr. Seth Stanfort had travelled where he listed, Miss Arcadia Walker where she willed. Their fancy had brought them both to this Greenland isle. Why should they have affected not to know each other? What more vulgar than to consider oneself bound by prejudices and foolish conventions? Having exchanged greetings with his companion, Mr. Seth Stanfort placed himself at her disposal, and the lady naturally accepted the service offered, without there being any further allusion between them to the meteorological phenomenon, the dénouement of which was at hand.

As the hours glided by, there was more and more excitement among the visitors to the island, and particularly among those who were principally interested in what was going to occur. Among these, of course, we include Mr. Dean Forsyth and Dr. Hudelson, since they persisted in their foolish claims.

"If only it will fall on the island!" was their constant prayer.

"And not outside!" mentally added the head of the Greenland Government.

"But not on our heads!" was the qualification of the more timid.

Too near or too far, these were the two extremes, in fact, to be feared.

The 16th and 17th of August passed without incident. Unluckily the weather changed for the worse, and the temperature began to fall considerably. It seemed as though the winter would be in advance. The mountains near the coast were already covered with snow; and, when the wind blew down from them, it was so biting and penetrating that everybody was glad to seek shelter in the warmer saloons of the vessels. No one had any wish to stay longer than was strictly necessary in such latitudes as these. As soon as they had contented their curiosity, they would willingly sail southwards once more.

Alone, perhaps, the two rivals, determined on upholding what they called their rights, would want to remain near their treasure. This might be expected of two such obstinates; and Francis, thinking of his dear Jenny, looked with grave disquietude on the prospect of their having to spend the winter in this inclement spot.

During the night between the 17th and 18th of August a storm swept over the Archipelago. Twenty hours previously the Boston astronomer had succeeded in getting a glimpse of the bolide, whose velocity was fast diminishing. But such was the violence of the storm that one wondered whether the bolide would not be carried away by it. No lull occurred throughout the 18th of August, and the early hours of the night were so troubled that the captains of the various vessels were seriously alarmed. However, towards midnight, the tempest began to decrease; and at five o'clock next morning all the passengers profited by the calmer weather to land. Was not this the 19th of August, the date fixed for the fall of the bolide?

It was time. At seven o'clock a hollow noise was heard, and a thud so tremendous was felt that the island shook on its base. A few moments later one of the natives ran to the house occupied by Monsieur de Schnack. He was the bearer of the great tidings.

The bolide had descended on the north-west point of the island of Upernivik.

XVIII

In which, in order to reach the bolide, Monsieur de Schnack and his numerous accomplices act the part of trespassers and burglars.

IMMEDIATELY there was a rush. Spread abroad in an instant, the news metamorphosed both tourists and natives. The vessels in the harbour were deserted by their crews, and a veritable human torrent flowed towards the spot indicated by the messenger.

If every one's attention had not been absorbed by the meteor, they might have remarked at the moment a fact which they would have been at a loss to explain. As if obeying some mysterious signal, one of the vessels anchored in the bay, a steamer whose funnel had been belching forth smoke since dawn, weighed anchor and sped out towards the open sea. She was a rakish-looking craft, and no doubt a swift one, for in a few minutes she had disappeared behind the cliffs.

Such behaviour was somewhat surprising. Why have come to Upernivik and quit it just when there was something to see? However, in the general hurry and scurry, no one noticed the departure, which, to say the least, was singular.

To go as quickly as they could, such was the one preoccupation of the crowd, composed not only of men, but of women and even children. They ran helter-skelter, hustling and jostling each other. To be just, we must except Mr. Seth Stanfort, who, as an old traveller, cool under any and every circumstance, preserved his tranquillity, and at first turned his back on the crowd to go and speak to Miss Arcadia Walker. Was it not natural to offer her his company in the excursion to see the bolide ?

"At last it has fallen, Mr. Stanfort!" were the words she greeted him with.

"At last it has fallen!" repeated her companion.

Indeed, this was the phrase in the mouths of all who were hurrying to the north-east point of the island. Five persons had managed to gain considerably over the main body, and to form a sort of vanguard. First there was Monsieur de Schnack, whose official position justified his having the premier place, next Messrs. Dean Forsyth and Hudelson marched abreast, with Francis and Jenny beside them. The young folks still continued to reverse their natural rôles, as they had on board the *Mozik*. Jenny showed herself ready to help Mr. Dean Forsyth, and Francis lent a succourable hand to Dr. Hudelson. Their obliging aid was not always well received, it must be owned; but, to tell the truth, the two rivals were so upset that they spoke without knowing what they said; and certainly they were incapable of interfering with the young couple, who took advantage of the situation to walk between them.

"The delegate will arrive ahead and take possession of the bolide," fulminated Mr. Forsyth.

"And will lay his grip upon it," added the doctor, fancying he was speaking to Francis Gordon.

"But that won't prevent me from asserting my rights!" proclaimed Mr. Dean Forsyth, addressing Jenny.

"No, indeed!" approved Dr. Sydney Hudelson, referring to his own.

It was some little satisfaction to Francis and Jenny to find the two astronomers forgetting their jealousy of each other in their common hatred of a third party.

At present the state of the atmosphere was, fortunately, modified. The tempest had entirely ceased, and the wind had veered round towards the south. If the sun rose only a few degrees above the horizon, it, nevertheless, shone through the clouds. There was no rain, no sharp wind; and the temperature was once more nearly up to fifty.

Between the station and the place to be reached a good league had to be covered. There were no vehicles at Upernivik, so, of course, all were on foot. Walking, indeed, as we have already said, was not difficult, save in the centre of the island and near the high shore cliffs. It was beyond these cliffs that the bolide had fallen, and for a while they hid the view. From the station the bolide was not visible. The native who had borne the tidings was now acting as guide. Behind him and the delegate, with the two rivals and Jenny and Francis, came Omicron, the Boston astronomer, and, last of all, the crowd of tourists. Mr. Seth Stanfort and Miss Arcadia Walker brought up the rear.

They neither of them were in ignorance of the rupture that had happened between the families of the two Whaston astronomers. Mr. Stanfort, in fact, had made Francis' acquaintance on board the *Mozik*, and the young man had told him all about the affair.

"The quarrel will be made up," prophesied Miss Arcadia, when she had the story related to her.

"It is to be wished," approved Mr. Stanfort.

"Yes," said Miss Arcadia, "and things will go on all the better after. You see, Mr. Stanfort, a few difficulties and anxieties are in keeping before marriage. Matches that are made too easily risk being unmade with the same facility! . . . Is not that your opinion ?"

"Quite, Miss Arcadia. For instance, our own

case proves it. Five minutes . . . on horseback . . . just time enough to take hands."

"And to loose them six weeks after," retorted Miss Arcadia Walker, smiling. "Well! Francis Gordon and Miss Jenny Hudelson will be all the surer of happiness for not marrying on horseback."

We need scarcely say that, during this conversation, both lady and gentleman had forgotten the bolide, and cared no more about it than Francis and Jenny, or than Judge Proth, whose genial, philosophic face must have occurred to their minds just then.

They were walking at a good pace over a plateau studded with meagre trees, whence birds fled more scared than they had ever been before in the environs of Upernivik. In half an hour two-thirds of the distance was covered. Nearly a mile more remained to be done before reaching the place where, according to the guide, the bolide lay. Paradoxical as such a statement seems, the tourists were obliged to rest awhile on account of the heat. They mopped the perspiration off their foreheads, just as if they had been in a warmer clime. Was it solely their exertions that caused them to be so hot? Partly, perhaps. But the air, too, was undoubtedly warmer. Where they were the temperature was certainly several degrees higher than at Upernivik. And the heat seemed to increase as they drew closer to their destination.

"Can the bolide's fall have altered the temperature of the archipelago?" asked Mr. Stanfort, laughing.

"It would be a good thing for the Greenlanders if it had!" replied Miss Arcadia in the same tone.

"It is probable that the block of gold, heated by its friction against the strata of the atmosphere, is still in an incandescent state," explained Mr. Wharf, the Boston astronomer, "and that the radiation of its heat is making itself felt here."

"Aha!" cried Mr. Seth Stanfort. "Must we wait, then, till it grows cool?"

"It would have got cool much quicker if it had fallen outside and not on the island," observed Francis Gordon to himself, returning to his favourite idea.

He was warm too; and Monsieur de Schnack and Mr. Wharf were perspiring, just as were the crowd of tourists, and the Greenlanders, who had never had such an experience before. After recovering their breaths, the party resumed their journey. Some five hundred yards farther on they reached the turn in the cliffs, and the meteor appeared in all its dazzling splendour.

Unfortunately, at the end of about two hundred yards they were all brought to a fresh full stop. This time it was not the heat which checked them, but an unexpected obstacle, the most unexpected obstacle that could have been met with in such a country. A fence made of stakes connected by

"PRIVATE PROPERTY. NO ROAD"

three rows of iron wire traced a huge curve right and left, and enclosed the district in front of them right down to the sea. Here and there some higher stakes had notice-boards on them, and, written in English, French, and Danish, was the same inscription. One of the boards was opposite Monsieur de Schnack, who read, to his amazement, "Private property. No road."

A private property in these far-off regions; this was something altogether extraordinary! On the sunny shores of the Mediterranean, or on the misty shores of the ocean, private country estates were understandable; but what could the owner do with this barren, rocky demesne? That, however, was not Monsieur de Schnack's business. Absurd or not, here was a private estate barring his way, and, in presence of the obstacle, his enthusiasm fell. An official delegate is naturally inclined to respect the principles on which civilized societies depend, and the inviolability of private domiciles is an axiom universally proclaimed.

Indeed, the owner here had taken good care to remind people, lest they should be tempted to forget this axiom. "No road" in three languages could not be misunderstood. Monsieur de Schnack was perplexed. To halt appeared exceedingly hard; and yet, on the other hand, was he to trespass on another man's property, in contempt of all laws divine and human?

Murmurs, growing louder every minute, were heard in the rear of the column, and these soon spread to the front. The hindmost ranks, unwitting of the cause that prevented them, protested with all the strength of their impatience. Being informed of what the obstacle was, they refused to be tranquillized, and their discontent becoming infectious, there arose a hubbub amidst which each individual in vain sought to get himself listened to. Were they going to stand still for ever before this fence? After travelling some thousands of miles to reach there, were they going to allow themselves to be stopped like fools by a wretched bit of iron wire? The owner of the land could not have the mad pretension to be also the owner of the meteor. He had, therefore, no good reason for not letting them pass. Anyway, if he were not willing to give them permission, it was easy enough to force their way through.

Whether these arguments of a summary kind shook Monsieur de Schnack's principles, or whether there was something besides, we are unable to say. However this might be, he took action. Just in front of him there was a gate fastened by a piece of string. With the help of his penknife he severed this string, and, without reflecting that the deed transformed him into a common trespasser and offender against the law, he entered the forbidden ground. Following him came the rest of the party, some jumping over the fence.

In a few instants, more than three thousand persons had invaded the "private property," making noisy comments, in the meanwhile, upon this strange occurrence.

But suddenly silence succeeded to the clamour. About a hundred yards beyond the fence, a small wooden hut, which had been hidden by a rise in the ground, came all at once into view; and at the door of this sorry dwelling, which had just opened, there stood a person of most bizarre aspect, who challenged the invaders!

"Hallo, there!" he cried in French, with harsh voice; "you are making yourselves at home and no mistake!"

Monsieur de Schnack understood French, and halted dead, an example which was imitated by all the tourists, who turned towards this bold challenge their three thousand puzzled faces.

XIX

In which Zephyrin Xirdal experiences an increasing aversion to the bolide, and what is the consequence of this aversion.

IF Zephyrin Xirdal had been alone, would he have come safely to his destination? Perhaps; for odder things have happened. None the less, one might have wagered against his doing so.

To tell the truth, nobody had laid any bets on the subject, since Zephyrin's good star had placed him under the safeguard of a mentor, whose practical mind neutralized the whims of this original. Zephyrin had no idea of what the difficulties were attending a journey to polar regions, since Monsieur Robert Lecœur had contrived to render it as simple as an excursion in the suburbs of Paris. At Havre, whither the express had conveyed them in a few hours, the two travellers were ushered on board a superb steamer, which immediately cast off from her moorings, and put out to sea without waiting for other passengers. As a matter of fact, the *Atlantic* was not an ordinary passenger-boat, but a yacht of between five and six hundred tons, which had been chartered by Monsieur Robert

Lecœur for their exclusive benefit. On account of the importance of the interests at stake, the banker had deemed it useful to have the means of communicating as he pleased with the civilized universe. Moreover, the huge profits he had already made by his speculation in mining shares allowed him to spend money like a prince; and he had secured this yacht, choosing it from among a hundred of the like sort in England.

The *Atlantic*, which had belonged to a multi-millionaire lord, was built for the purpose of fast sailing. With its elongated and strong yet slender framework, it was capable, under the impetus of its four thousand horse-power engine, of attaining and even exceeding twenty knots. Monsieur Lecœur's choice had been dictated by this particularity, which, in case of need, would be of inestimable service to him.

Zephyrin Xirdal manifested no surprise at thus having a vessel at his orders. Perhaps, indeed, he did not notice this detail. At any rate, he crossed the deck and installed himself in his cabin without formulating the slightest observation.

The distance between Havre and Upernivik is about eight hundred sea-leagues, which the *Atlantic*, steaming at full speed, could have covered in six days. But Monsieur Lecœur, being in no hurry, occupied about twelve days on the voyage, and they arrived off the station of Upernivik only in the evening of the 18th of July. During these twelve days Zephyrin scarcely opened his mouth. At meals, when they were necessarily together, the banker tried time and again to turn the conversation to the object of their voyage, but could never obtain any answer. In vain he spoke to him of the meteor; his godson seemed to have completely forgotten it, and no gleam of intelligence lighted up his lack-lustre eyes.

For the moment Xirdal was looking inside himself, and was pursuing the solution of other problems. What were they? He told no one. But, in some manner, they must have had to do with the sea; for, standing either in the fore or the aft of the yacht, he spent his hours gazing at the waves. Perhaps one might suppose he was continuing his investigations as to the phenomenon of superficial tension concerning which he had said a few words to the people passing him in the street, believing he was talking to his friend Marcel Leroux. Perhaps, too, the deductions he then drew were connected with the marvellous inventions with which he was subsequently to astonish the world.

On the morrow of their arrival at Upernivik, Monsieur Lecœur, who was beginning to despair, tried to arouse his godson from his reverie by placing before him his machine, which had been stripped of its protecting envelope. He had calculated rightly. As soon as the machine was perceived Zephyrin shook himself, as if he were awaking from sleep, and stared about him with eyes that had recovered their utmost firmness of look and their greatest lucidity.

"Where are we?" he asked.

"At Upernivik," replied Monsieur Lecœur.

"And my piece of land?"

"We are going to it."

This was not quite true. Previously they had to call on Monsieur Biarn Haldorsen, Chief Surveyor for the North, whose residence was easily found by means of the flag that was above it. After an exchange of polite greetings, business negotiations were opened through an interpreter prudently provided by the banker.

A first difficulty arose directly. Not that Monsieur Biarn Haldorsen was inclined to contest the property title that was submitted to him. It was the interpretation which was not clear. By the terms of the deed of sale, which was quite in order and bore every official signature and seal requisite, the Greenland Government, represented by its diplomatic agent at Copenhagen, ceded to Monsieur Zephyrin Xirdal a surface of nine square kilometres bounded by four equal sides of three kilometres each, situated according to the four cardinal points, and cutting each other at right angles at a similar distance from a central point located in 72° 51′ 30″ north latitude and 55° 35′ 18″ west longitude, the whole for a sum of five hundred kroner per square kilometre, making a total amount of just over six thousand francs.

Monsieur Biarn Haldorsen was quite disposed to acquiesce and to recognize the deed of sale; but where was the central point? Forsooth, he was not ignorant of longitude and latitude, but these things were no more than words to him. Had he been told that latitude was an animal or a vegetable, and longitude a mineral or a piece of furniture, the statement would have seemed plausible; he had no particular preference.

Zephyrin Xirdal in a few words completed the cosmographic knowledge required in the Chief Surveyor, and next proceeded, himself, to make, with the help of the *Atlantic's* instruments, the necessary observations and reckonings. The captain of a Danish ship that was then in the harbour could, he said, check the results and fully reassure his Excellency, Monsieur Biarn Haldorsen. This was done.

In two days Zephyrin Xirdal had finished his work, the accuracy of which was certified to by the said Danish captain; and now the second difficulty presented itself. The point of terrestrial surface whose co-ordinates were 72° 51′ 30″ north latitude and 55° 35′ 18″ west longitude, was discovered to be in the sea, about two hundred and fifty yards northwards of the island of Upernivik.

Dismayed by this discovery, Monsieur Lecœur

broke out into violent recriminations. What were they going to do? It appeared they had come into these far-off regions to see the bolide take a bath. Was such negligence possible? How could Zephyrin Xirdal have been guilty of such an egregious error?

The explanation of this error was simple enough. Zephyrin did not know that the word Upernivik designated not only a village, but an island. After mathematically determining the place of the bolide's fall, he had trusted to a poor map in a school atlas—the map he now took from his pocket and showed to the irritated banker. This map indicated correctly enough that the point of the globe situated in 72° 51′ 30″ north latitude and 55° 35′ 18″ west longitude was near the village of Upernivik, but it neglected to indicate that the village, instead of lying inland, was on the island of the same name, close to the sea. Zephyrin, without verifying, had relied on this too rough-and-ready map.

May this mistake he made serve as a lesson! May readers of this narrative devote themselves to the study of geography, and not forget, above all, that Upernivik is an island! It will be useful to them if perchance they happen to have a bolide to receive worth the number of milliards we have quoted in a preceding chapter! Unfortunately, there was this Whaston bolide to receive under parlous circumstances!

If the land could have been mapped out a little more to the south, the trickery would have been advantageous to the purchaser, in case of the meteor's deviation. But Zephyrin Xirdal having committed the imprudence to complete his Excellency Monsieur Biarn Haldorsen's education, and to accept a verification at present troublesome, it was no longer possible to rectify the bargain, which had to be taken as it was. Their purchase consequently comprised both land and sea.

The southern limit of the land portion—which was the more interesting of the two—was found on examination to comprise twelve hundred and fifty-one yards of the northern shore of Upernivik; the length of three kilometres exceeding the breadth of the island in this part carried the east and west boundaries out into the open sea. In reality, therefore, Zephyrin Xirdal obtained rather more than a square mile of land in lieu of the nine square kilometres that he had bought. From a monetary point of view the bargain was a bad one.

From the special point of view of the bolide's fall, the bargain indeed was a shocking one. The spot that Zephyrin had so cleverly computated was in the sea. True, he had allowed for deviations, since he had taken in a radius of fifteen hundred yards round this spot. But the question was on what side the deviation would happen, if it did? And this he did not know. While the meteor might fall in the restricted land portion remaining to him, it might also fall outside. Monsieur Lecœur was deeply perplexed.

"What are you going to do now?" he asked his godson.

The latter raised his arms in token of ignorance.

"We must do something, anyway," said the banker angrily. "You must get us out of this mess."

Zephyrin reflected an instant.

"The first thing," he replied at length, "is to fence in the land, and to build a hut that can lodge us. I will see to the rest."

Monsieur Lecœur set to work. Within a week the sailors of the *Atlantic*, assisted by a few Greenlanders that were tempted by the high wages offered, constructed an iron wire fence, the two ends of which went down to the sea; and built a log hut, which was provided with the furniture most needful.

On the 26th of July, three weeks before the day on which the bolide was to fall, Zephyrin set himself to his task. After making some observations of the meteor in the upper zones of the atmosphere, he soared into the upper zones of mathematics. His fresh calculations served only to prove the correctness of those he had previously carried out. No mistake had been made, no deviation had occurred. The bolide would fall exactly at the spot predicted, namely, in 72° 51′ 30″ north latitude, and 55° 35′ 18″ west longitude.

"Consequently in the sea," said Monsieur Lecœur, hiding his wrath with difficulty.

"In the sea, evidently," said Xirdal serenely. As a true mathematician, he experienced no other sentiment than satisfaction to find how extremely exact his calculations had been. But almost immediately he was struck by the other aspect of the affair.

"The deuce!" he exclaimed, with a changed voice, and looking at his godfather hesitatingly.

Monsieur Lecœur tried to keep calm.

"Come, Zephyrin," he said, in a tone adopted when speaking to children. "I suppose we are not going to sit still and fold our arms. There has been a blunder; it must be repaired. Since you were able to act on the bolide when it was right up in the sky, you can surely cause it to deviate a few hundred yards now that it is nearer the earth. The thing must be child's play."

"Ah! so you think that, do you?" answered Zephyrin, shaking his head. "When I acted on the meteor, it was four hundred kilometres off. At that distance the earth's attraction was exercised in such a manner that the quantity of energy I projected on one of its faces was able to cause an appreciable rupture of equilibrium. Now the case is no longer the same. The bolide is nearer, and the earth's attraction is so strong that a little more or a little less force will not alter the position much. On the other hand, if the bolide's absolute velocity has diminished, its angular velocity has much increased; and it is passing at present like lightning into the most convenient inclination for falling, so that there is scarcely any time to influence it."

"Then you can do nothing?" queried Monsieur Lecœur, biting his lips to prevent himself from exploding.

"I didn't say that," corrected Xirdal. "The thing is not easy. But we can try."

He did try; and with such good effect that, on the 17th of August, he considered the success of his experiment as certain. The bolide had been deviated and would fall on *terra firma*, about fifty yards from the shore, a distance sufficient to maintain it from escaping.

Unluckily the tempest that raged during the couple of days following swept all the surface of the ground, and Xirdal had good reason to fear that the bolide's trajectory might be affected by such a displacement of air. As we have already said, the storm dropped during the night between the 18th and 19th; but the two inhabitants of the hut did not avail themselves of the lull to take any rest. After watching the sun set, at rather more than half-past ten in the evening, they waited and saw it rise again less than three hours later in a sky almost entirely free of clouds. The fall occurred exactly at the hour announced by Zephyrin. At fifty-seven minutes thirty-five seconds past six a fulgurous light rent the atmosphere towards the north, half blinding Monsieur Lecœur and his godson, who for the last hour had been gazing at the horizon from their doorstep. Almost at the same moment, a hollow noise was heard and the ground shook under the formidable shock. The meteor had fallen.

When Zephyrin Xirdal and Monsieur Lecœur recovered the use of their eyes, what they perceived was the block of gold some five hundred yards away.

"It is burning," faltered the banker, overcome by his emotion.

"Yes," replied Zephyrin, incapable of uttering more than this monosyllable.

Little by little, however, they regained their self-possession and were able to realize better what they saw.

As a matter of fact, the bolide was in an incandescent state. Its temperature must have been more than a thousand degrees, almost at melting-point. Its porous composition was clearly visible, and the Greenwich Observatory had been quite right in comparing it to a sponge. Traversing the surface, whose cooling, due to radiation, darkened its hue, an infinite number of chinks and crevices allowed the eye to penetrate into the interior, where the metal was red-hot. Intersecting each other, and twisted into a thousand zig-zags, these crevices formed alveoli whence the hot air escaped, hissing.

Although the bolide had been considerably flattened in its swift descent, its spherical shape was still preserved. The higher portion was fairly round, while the bottom, being crushed, fitted into the anfractuosities of the shore.

"I believe it is slipping into the sea!" cried Monsieur Lecœur at the end of a few minutes.

His godson remained silent.

"You told me it would fall fifty yards away from the seaside!" added the banker.

"It is ten yards clear at the centre," replied Zephyrin. "You are forgetting the half of its diameter."

"Ten are not fifty."

"The storm has caused it to deviate."

The two interlocutors became silent once more, and continued gazing at the meteor.

To tell the truth, Monsieur Lecœur's fears were not without cause. The bolide was on the slope of the cliff, and, having a radius of fifty-five metres, as the Greenwich Observatory had affirmed, its farther hemisphere projected forty-five yards over the sea. The enormous mass of metal, already softened by heat, had sagged on the seaward side, and its lower portions hung down almost into the water. The other hemisphere, however, rooted in the rock, held fast and kept the whole from slipping.

It did not slip because the aggregate mass was in equilibrium. But the equilibrium was unstable, and a very small impetus would suffice to send the golden treasure down into the ocean's depths. There needed only an initial movement and nothing thenceforward could restrain it.

"All the more reason for hurrying up," said Monsieur Lecœur to himself, as he reflected. It was absurd to be losing time in contemplation, to the detriment of his interests. Hastening behind the hut, he ran up the French flag to the top of a mast high enough for the colours to be perceived by the vessels anchored in front of Upernivik. As we have related already, the signal was understood and obeyed. The *Atlantic* immediately steamed off towards the nearest telegraph station, from where a cable was sent to Lecœur's bank in Paris. The telegram was in cipher, and informed those who received it as follows: "Bolide fallen; sell."

In Paris the order would be executed without delay, and would again bring Monsieur Lecœur huge profits, since he knew what he was about. When the bolide's fall was announced, mining shares would undergo a final slump, and the banker would then buy up again in most favourable terms. At any rate, he could not fail to gather in a respectable number of million francs.

Untouched by these vulgar interests, Zephyrin Xirdal stood absorbed in his contemplation, when suddenly his ear was assailed by a loud murmur of voices. Turning round, he perceived the crowd of tourists who, with Monsieur de Schnack at their head, had ventured to trespass on his land. Ah! this was intolerable. Having purchased a place where he could be his own master, Zephyrin was revolted by such impertinence. With rapid steps he walked to meet these intruders. The delegate of the Greenland Government spared him half of the journey.

"How is it, sir," said Xirdal, addressing him, "that you are trespassing on my land? Didn't you see the notice-boards?"

"Excuse me, sir," answered Monsieur de Schnack politely, "we saw the notice-boards, but thought that, under such exceptional circumstances, we might be allowed to disobey."

"Exceptional circumstances? . . ." questioned Xirdal innocently. "What exceptional circumstances?"

Monsieur de Schnack was in turn astonished.

"What exceptional circumstances? . . ." he repeated. "Must I then inform you, sir, that the Whaston bolide has just fallen on this island?"

"I know that," said Xirdal. "But there is nothing exceptional about it. The fall of a bolide is common enough."

"Not when it is in gold."

"Whether it's in gold or anything else, a bolide is a bolide."

"Such is not the opinion of these ladies and gentlemen," replied Monsieur de Schnack, pointing to the crowd of tourists, most of whom did not understand a word of the dialogue. "All these people have come here on purpose to see the Whaston bolide fall. You will own that it would have been hard for them, after such a journey, to be stopped by a wire fence."

"That's true," said Xirdal, now disposed to be conciliatory.

Things were therefore assuming a better aspect, when Monsieur de Schnack was imprudent enough to add :

"As far as I am personally concerned, I could scarcely allow myself to be checked by your fence, since I am invested with an official duty."

"What duty ?"

"To take possession of the bolide in the name of Greenland, whose representative here I am."

Xirdal gave a start.

"To take possession of the bolide !" he cried. "You are mad, my dear sir."

"I fail to see why," retorted Monsieur de Schnack in an offended tone. "The bolide has fallen on the territory of Greenland. It consequently belongs to the State of Greenland, since it is no one's private property."

"You are entirely mistaken," protested Zephyrin Xirdal. "First of all, the bolide has not fallen on the territory of Greenland, but on mine, seeing that Greenland has sold it to me in return for hard cash. Moreover, the bolide belongs to some one already, and that some one is myself."

"You ?"

"Yes, me."

"On what grounds ?"

"On all grounds, my dear sir. But for me the bolide would still be circling in space, where you, representative as you may be, would find it difficult to seize. Why shouldn't it be mine, since it is on my land and I made it fall here ?"

"What ?" exclaimed Monsieur de Schnack.

"I say that I made it fall here. Indeed, I took the precaution to send information of the fact to the International Conference that has met, it seems, at Washington. I expect my telegram has interrupted the sittings."

Monsieur de Schnack stared doubtfully at his interlocutor. Was he a fool or a madman ?

"Sir," he replied, "I was one of the delegates sitting at the International Conference, and I can assure you that the Conference was continuing its labours when I quitted Washington. On the other hand, I can likewise assure you that I never heard of the telegram you say you sent."

Monsieur de Schnack was telling the truth. Somewhat hard of hearing, he had not caught a word of the telegram, which was read, as is customary in every Parliament that respects itself, amidst the din of private conversations.

"Nevertheless, I sent it," declared Zephyrin Xirdal, who was beginning to get excited. "Whether it reached its destination or not does not affect the question of my rights."

"Your rights? . . ." retorted Monsieur de Schnack, who was also getting angry in the course of this unexpected discussion. "Do you dare seriously to put forward claims to the bolide?"

"Why not?" asked Xirdal sarcastically.

"A bolide worth so many milliards!"

"What difference does that make? If it were worth milliards of billions and trillions, that would not hinder its being mine."

"Yours? . . . you are jesting. . . . A man to possess alone more gold than all the rest of the world besides! . . . It would not be tolerable."

"I don't know whether it's tolerable or not," cried Zephyrin Xirdal, now thoroughly angry. "I know only one thing, the bolide is mine."

"We shall see," concluded Monsieur de Schnack shortly. "For the present, you will be good enough to let us go on our way."

So saying, the delegate raised his hat, and, at a sign from him, the native guide set off in advance. Monsieur de Schnack followed him, and all the tourists followed Monsieur de Schnack.

Planted on his long legs, Zephyrin Xirdal watched the crowd walk by which seemed to ignore him. His indignation was great. To trespass on his property and behave as if they were in a conquered country! And then to contest his rights! It was more than a joke. However, there was nothing to be done against such a crowd. So, when the last stranger had gone by, he was constrained to retreat to his hut. But if he was vanquished, he was not convinced, and as he went he gave free vent to his feelings.

"It's disgusting . . . disgusting!" he repeated, gesticulating like a railway signal.

Meanwhile the crowd was hastening after the guide, who halted at last, being unable to go farther. Monsieur de Schnack and Mr. Wharf joined him, and then Messrs. Forsyth and Hudelson, Francis, Jenny, Omicron, Mr. Seth Stanfort, and Mrs. Arcadia Walker, and the rest of the sightseers who had been brought to the shore of Baffin Bay. Yes, they could not go any farther. The heat, which was insupportable, forbade another step.

Besides, it would have been useless. Less than four hundred yards away, the sphere of gold showed itself, and everybody could contemplate it, as Zephyrin Xirdal and Monsieur Lecœur had contemplated it an hour before. It no longer radiated as when it traced its orbit in space; but such was its lustre that their eyes could scarcely bear it. In fine, after being intangible up in the sky, it was no less intangible now that it lay on the earth's surface.

In this spot the shore formed a sort of round plateau, one of those rocks designated by the name *unalek* in the tongue of the natives. Sloping towards the sea, it ended in a cliff that rose sheer above the water-level to a height of thirty yards. Here it was that the bolide lay.

"Twenty yards farther," murmured Francis Gordon, as he looked, "and it would have gone to the bottom. . . ."

"And to get it up again would have been fishing extraordinary," added Miss Arcadia Walker.

"Monsieur de Schnack has not got it even now," remarked Mr. Seth Stanfort. "Some time will have to elapse before the Greenland Government can put it into their coffers."

True, but this was only a matter of time and patience. With the approach of the arctic winter the cooling was inevitable.

Mr. Dean Forsyth and Dr. Sydney Hudelson stood there, motionless, as if hypnotized by this mass of gold that scorched their eyes. Both had tried to move nearer, and both had been obliged to draw back, as well as the impatient Omicron, who had a narrow escape of being roasted like a joint of beef. At this distance of four hundred yards, the temperature was nigh on a hundred and twenty degrees Fahrenheit, and the

At this distance of four hundred yards

heat given off by the meteor rendered the air unbreathable.

"Anyway . . . it was there . . . it lay on the island. . . . It was not at the bottom of the sea. . . . It was not lost for everybody. . . . It was in the hands of lucky Greenland. . . . All that was required was to wait."

This was what the inquisitive sightseers said to themselves as they watched in the suffocating atmosphere near the cliff.

Yes, wait. . . . But how long? Would it not take a month, even two, for the bolide to cool? Such masses of metal heated to a high temperature could remain incandescent for a long time. Examples had been furnished already by meteorites of much less volume.

Three hours went by and no one had manifested any intention of leaving the spot. Were they waiting to see if they could get nearer to the bolide? At any rate, they wouldn't be able to make the attempt to-day, or to-morrow. Unless they established a camp there, and had provisions brought, they would be obliged to return to their vessels.

"Mr. Stanfort," said Miss Arcadia Walker, "do you think the cooling is a question of hours only?"

"Neither of hours nor of days only, Miss Walker."

"Then I am going back to the *Oregon*; it will be easy to come here again."

"You are quite right," answered Mr. Stanfort; "and, imitating your example, I will make my way in the direction of the *Mozik*. I fancy it must be lunch-time."

It was the wisest thing to do; but this wise thing did not commend itself to Messrs. Forsyth and Hudelson and Francis, and Jenny tried in vain to persuade them. The crowd melted slowly away, and Monsieur de Schnack at length decided to retrace his steps to Upernivik. Yet still the two foolish men persisted in staying to feast their eyes on their meteor.

"Aren't you coming, father?" asked Jenny for the dozenth time towards two o'clock in the afternoon.

The doctor's only reply was to go a few steps nearer the bolide and to retreat precipitately on the instant. It was as if he had ventured in front of an open furnace. Mr. Dean Forsyth, who had trotted forward also, was compelled to right about face with no less rapidity.

"Come, uncle; come, Dr. Hudelson," said Francis, in his turn; "it is time we got back on board. . . . Zounds! the bolide won't run away now. Feasting your eyes on it won't fill your stomachs."

All efforts were useless. Not till evening, when they were worn out with fatigue and hunger, did Mr. Forsyth and Dr. Hudelson resign themselves to leave the spot, with a firm determination to return on the morrow. They returned, indeed, at an early hour, but only to find the place guarded by fifty armed men—the entire Greenland military force—who kept spectators at a respectable distance from the precious meteor.

Against whom had the Government taken this precaution? Against Zephyrin Xirdal? If so, fifty men were too many. The more so as the bolide defended itself very well alone. Even the boldest person would hardly have been able to get a yard nearer than the day before. At this rate, months would elapse before Monsieur de Schnack would be able to enter into effective possession of the treasure in Greenland's name. Anyway, the bolide was under surveillance. With so many milliards at stake, it was deemed there could not be too much prudence.

At Monsieur de Schnack's request, one of the vessels in the roads had sailed to announce the great tidings by telegraph to the world at large. Within forty-eight hours, the bolide's fall would be officially known everywhere. Would not this upset Monsieur Lecœur's plans? In no wise. The departure of the *Atlantic* had taken place twenty-four hours beforehand; and, since the yacht's speed was incontestably superior, the banker disposed of thirty-six hours' advance in which to carry out successfully his financial speculation.

If the Government representatives of Greenland had put the fifty guards in proximity to the meteor simply lest some one should run away with it, they must have been doubly reassured when, in the afternoon of the same day, they found there were seventy men exercising surveillance. Towards midday a cruiser had anchored off Upernivik. At her masthead waved the stars and stripes of the United States of America. No sooner had the anchor been cast than twenty men had disembarked, under the command of a midshipman, and were now encamped in the neighbourhood of the bolide.

When Monsieur de Schnack heard of this increase to the guard, he experienced feelings that were somewhat mingled. Though pleased to know that the treasure was being protected with such zeal, this landing of American marines on Greenland's territory caused him a certain amount of uneasiness. The midshipman, to whom he went for information, was not able to satisfy him. This officer was obeying orders and had nothing further to communicate.

Monsieur de Schnack resolved to lodge a complaint on the morrow with the captain of the cruiser; but, when he was about to carry his purpose out, he found that he would have to lodge two. During the night a second cruiser, this time an English one, had arrived. The captain, on being apprised of the bolide's fall, had imitated the example of his American colleague and likewise landed twenty marines, who, under the guidance of a second midshipman, had proceeded at a quick march towards the north-west of the island.

Monsieur de Schnack was in a quandary. What did it all mean? And his perplexities were bound to augment as the hours went by. In the afternoon a third cruiser was signalled, which was flying the tricolour flag; and, a couple of hours later, twenty French sailors, under the command of a second lieutenant, landed to strengthen the guard that was being maintained over the bolide.

The situation was becoming decidedly involved. In the night of the 21st to the 22nd, there was a fourth arrival, that of a Russian cruiser. Then, during the day of the 22nd, came successively a Japanese vessel, an Italian, and a German one. On the morrow, an Argentine cruiser and a Spanish one appeared, to be followed shortly afterwards by three other vessels, one Chilian, one Portuguese, and one Dutch.

On the 25th of August, sixteen men-of-war, amidst which the *Atlantic* had quietly returned to anchor, formed, in front of Upernivik, an international squadron such as these hyperborean regions had never seen. And, each of the vessels having disembarked its twenty men under the command of an officer, there were now three hundred and twenty marines and sixteen officers of all nationalities on a soil that the fifty Greenlander soldiers, in spite of their courage, would not have been able to defend.

Each vessel had some particular piece of news to bring, and the news was not very satisfactory, judging from its effect. If it was patent that the International Conference was continuing its sittings, it was no less evident that the continuation was purely a matter of form. Thenceforward the question was a diplomatic one, and—this was added privately—a military one. The various Foreign Offices were busy discussing with each other, and the language employed was not altogether suave. As the number of vessels increased, reports became disquieting. Nothing definite was known; but rumours circulated among the officers and crews, and gradually relations grew more strained between each and all of the contingents on shore. If the American Commodore had at first invited his English colleague to dine, and the latter, on returning his compliment, had profited by the opportunity to render cordial homage to the French captain, these international courtesies soon ended. At present each party remained secluded, waiting to regulate their conduct according to the way in which the wind should blow; and there were premonitory symptoms of a hurricane.

Meantime Zephyrin Xirdal refused to be appeased. His godfather was tired of his recriminations, and wearied out in vain attempts to appeal to his common-sense.

"You must understand, my dear Zephyrin, that Monsieur de Schnack is right," he said to him, "and that it is impossible to let a single person dispose of such a colossal sum. The intervention is quite natural. But let me do what I want. When the first excitement is past I will intervene, in my turn, and I don't think it will be possible for them not to allow the justice of our cause. I shall obtain something, certainly."

"Something!" cried Xirdal. "Pooh! a fig for your something. What do I want with the gold? What should I do with it?"

"Then why do you make such a fuss?" objected Mr. Lecœur.

"Because the bolide is mine. I am indignant any one should try to take it. I won't stand such conduct."

"What can you do against all the world, my poor Zephyrin?"

"If only I knew, I should soon do it. But patience! . . . When this fool of a delegate put forward his claim to my bolide, the behaviour was bad enough. What is to be said to-day? . . . At present there are as many robbers as there are countries. Not to mention that they are going to fall out among themselves, as I hear. Why the deuce didn't I leave the bolide where it was? Getting it to fall seemed a joke to me.

I found the experiment interesting. . . . If I had been aware! Poor devils that haven't ten halfpence in their pockets are going to fight now over milliards! You can say what you like, I'm more and more disgusted."

Xirdal refused to look at the affair in any other light. At any rate, he was wrong to be irritated with Monsieur de Schnack. The unfortunate delegate, to use a familiar expression, was also in a bit of a fix. This invasion of Greenland's territory was not of good augury to him; and the Republic's prodigious fortune appeared to him to rest on foundations that were exceedingly unsafe. What, however, could he do? Could he, with his fifty men, drive the three hundred and twenty foreign marines into the sea, and cannon, torpedo, and sink the sixteen mammoth ironclads that surrounded him?

It was clear that he could not. No, all he was able to do and ought to do was to protest in his country's name against the violation of the national territory.

One day, when the two captains of the English and French vessels had come on shore, out of curiosity, Monsieur de Schnack seized the occasion to ask for explanations and to make official representations which, while diplomatically moderate, were none the less energetic. The English captain replied. Monsieur de Schnack, he said, was wrong to take them to task. The officers in charge of the vessels in the roads were merely conforming themselves to the orders of their respective Admiralties. They had neither to discuss nor to quibble about these orders, but only to carry them out. However, it might be presumed that the international disembarkment of troops had no other object than the maintenance of quietness and tranquillity in presence of so many people, whose numbers, indeed, it had been anticipated would have been still greater. In any case, Monsieur de Schnack need not be alarmed. The question was being deliberated upon, and the rights of each would undoubtedly be respected.

"Very good!" approved the French captain.

"Since all rights will be respected, I shall be able, then, to defend mine," suddenly cried a gentleman, unceremoniously interrupting the conversation.

"Whom have I the honour . . . ?" questioned the English captain.

"Mr. Dean Forsyth, astronomer, Whaston, the legitimate owner of the bolide," replied the interrupter pompously, whilst Monsieur de Schnack gave a slight shrug.

"Oh, indeed!" answered the captain. "I am quite familiar with your name, Mr. Forsyth. . . . Of course, if you have rights, you should be enabled to defend them."

"Rights!" exclaimed, at this moment, a second interrupter. "Then what am I to say of mine?

Was it not I alone, Dr. Sydney Hudelson, who first drew the attention of the universe to the bolide?"

"You!" protested Mr. Dean Forsyth, turning as if he had been stung by a viper.

"Yes, I."

"A mere quack pretend to have made such a discovery!"

"Quite as well as an ignoramus like you!"

"A braggart who does not even know how to look through a telescope!"

"A merry-andrew who doesn't know what a telescope is!"

"I not know!"

"I a quack!"

"I'm not so ignorant that I don't know how to unmask an impostor!"

"I'm not so much of a quack that I can't convict a thief!"

"Oh! this is too much!" foamed Mr. Dean Forsyth. "Take care, sir!"

The two rivals, with blazing eyes and clenched fists, were threatening to attack each other; and the scene would probably have finished badly if Francis and Jenny had not rushed in between the adversaries.

"Uncle!" cried Francis, restraining Mr. Dean Forsyth with vigorous hand.

"Father! I beg you . . . Father!" exclaimed Jenny, all in tears.

"Who are these two mad folk?" asked Zephyrin

Xirdal, who happened to be watching from some little distance this tragi-comical incident, with Mr. Seth Stanfort near him.

When out travelling it is easy to break through conventionalities. Mr. Seth Stanfort, therefore, though not acquainted with Zephyrin, replied to the question.

"You must have heard of Mr. Dean Forsyth and Dr. Sydney Hudelson," he said.

"The two amateur astronomers of Whaston?"

"Yes."

"The discoverers of the bolide that has fallen here?"

"Yes."

"Why are they quarrelling?"

"They can't agree as to who discovered it first."

Zephyrin shrugged his shoulders contemptuously.

"What nonsense!"

"And they both claim to be the owners of the bolide," continued Mr. Seth Stanfort.

"Simply because they happened to see it in the sky?"

"Yes."

"They have a cheek," pronounced Zephyrin. "But this young man and this girl, what have they to do with the business?"

Obligingly Mr. Seth Stanfort explained the situation. He related under what circumstances the two betrothed had been compelled to defer their wedding, and how the two families had been separated by this absurd jealousy which kept the couple apart. Xirdal seemed thunderstruck. He looked at Mr. Dean Forsyth held back by Francis Gordon, and at Dr. Hudelson struggling in the weaker arms of his daughter Jenny, and studied them as if they had been some new zoological specimens. When Mr. Seth Stanfort had terminated his narration, Zephyrin did not thank him, but came out instead with a vigorous: "This is really too much!" and strode away. The narrator stared calmly after the disappearing original; then, without bestowing any further thought upon him, joined Miss Arcadia Walker, who, during the dialogue, had been, for a wonder, neglected.

Zephyrin Xirdal was extremely angry. Wrenching open the door of his hut, he burst in upon his godfather.

"Uncle," he said to Monsieur Lecœur with a voice that made the gentleman start, "I do declare it's too disgusting."

"What is it now?" asked the banker.

"Zounds! this bolide!"

"What has the bolide done now?"

"It's devastating the earth, that's what it's doing. Its crimes are already too numerous to mention. Not content with transforming all these people into robbers, it's in a fair way to ruin the world with fire and sword. And that's not all. It's trying its best now to make lovers fall out. Go and look at this girl, uncle, and tell me what you think. She'd make a milestone cry. Decidedly it's all too disgusting."

"What lovers? What girl are you speaking of? What's this new whim of yours?" asked Monsieur Lecœur, bewildered.

Zephyrin Xirdal did not deign to reply.

"Yes, it's too disgusting," he repeated with emphasis. "But it shan't go on like that. I'll set 'em all in agreement, and sharply, too."

"What stupid trick are you meditating now, Zephyrin?"

"Gad! a very simple one. I'll shove their bolide into the sea."

Monsieur Lecœur leaped to his feet. His face had paled under the shock, which stopped his heart beating. He was only too well aware that this was not a mere angry threat, and that Xirdal was quite capable of executing what he had said.

"You won't do it, Zephyrin," begged the banker.

"On the contrary, I shall do it. Nothing will prevent me. I've had enough, and I'm going to set about the thing at once."

"But just reflect, blockhead . . ."

Monsieur Lecœur cut short what he had begun to say. A splendid idea had just flashed across his mind. In a few seconds more his financier's brain had examined the pros and cons of it.

"Why not?" he murmured.

After a moment's further thought, he was confirmed in his approval of the plan that had occurred to him. Addressing Zephyrin, he said:

"I won't oppose you any longer. You mean to drive the bolide into the sea. All right. But can't you allow me a few days' respite?"

The banker spoke in a decided tone, and like a man who was in a hurry and had much to do in a short space of time.

"I am obliged to wait for a very good reason," answered Xirdal. "The machine will want altering a little for the purpose of the work I am going to do. Probably the alterations will require five or six days."

"That will bring us, then, to the 3rd of September?"

"Yes."

"Good!" said Monsieur Lecœur, and he left the hut and walked rapidly in the direction of Upernivik, while his godson set to work.

Without losing any time, the banker proceeded to board the *Atlantic,* whose funnel began immediately to belch forth clouds of black smoke. Two hours later, the banker having returned to the shore, the *Atlantic* was ploughing her way through the sea and soon disappeared behind the horizon.

Like everything else which is characterized by genius, Monsieur Lecœur's plan was sublime in its simplicity. He had two alternatives to choose from. Either he must denounce his godson to the international troops, or he must let things take their course. Monsieur Lecœur adopted the second. Had he adopted the first, he might have reasonably counted on the gratitude of the various governments interested in the matter; and no doubt a share would have been assigned him of the treasure thus saved by his intervention. But what share? A small one, in all likelihood, rendered still more insignificant by the depreciation of gold which the bolide's utilization must inevitably cause. If, on the contrary, he kept silence, besides suppressing all the different calamities which this maleficent mass of gold carried as an embryon in its womb, and which it was about to spread, like a devastating torrent, over the surface of the earth, he avoided the inconveniences that were personal to himself, and assured himself solid advantages into the bargain. Being the only person who for the next five days would have possession of this secret, he was free to take advantage of it. For this he had simply to despatch a fresh cable, with the help of the *Atlantic*, to be interpreted at the Rue Drouot as follows: "A sensational event imminent. Buy mining shares in unlimited quantity."

This order would be easily executed. The bolide's fall being known everywhere at present, mining shares were down to almost nothing. No doubt they were being offered everywhere without finding purchasers. What a boom there would be when the end of the adventure was known! With what rapidity the shares would rise to their previous rates, to the great profit of their fortunate holder!

We may here say that Monsieur Lecœur's anticipations were justified. The telegram was duly received at the Rue Drouot Bank, and the banker's instructions were acted upon the same day at the Bourse. All the mining shares offered on 'Change were bought up by Lecœur's bank, and on the morrow the like operation was repeated. What a harvest in the two days! Smaller mining shares were obtained at a few centimes per share, and shares formerly of greater importance and now quoted at two and three francs, and shares of tip-top quality depreciated to ten and twelve francs—all were gathered in indiscriminately.

At the end of forty-eight hours the news of these purchases began to be known on the various Exchanges of the world, and created no little sensation. Lecœur's bank, having a reputation for being wideawake, could hardly be acting recklessly in thus monopolizing a special category of values. There was some mystery in the matter; and, this being the general sentiment, higher rates resulted. But it was too late. The speculation had succeeded. Monsieur Robert Lecœur now held more than half the gold production of the globe in his hands.

While these things were happening in Paris, Zephyrin Xirdal was turning to account, with a view to altering his machine, the several accessories he had taken care to provide himself with before quitting Paris. Inside he connected wires together in intricate circuits. Outside he added bulbs of strange form, placing them in the centre of two new reflectors. At the date fixed, namely, on the 3rd of September, everything was complete, and Zephyrin announced that he was ready to commence. The presence of his godfather exceptionally assured him a real, instead of an imaginary audience. The opportunity was an excellent one to show his talents as a speaker, and he availed himself of it.

"My machine," he said, as he closed the circuit, "has nothing incomprehensible or diabolical about it. Its one quality is that of being an organ of transformation. It receives electricity in its ordinary form and gives it back under a higher form that I myself have discovered. This bulb that you see, and that now begins to whirl round like mad, is the one I used in order to attract the bolide. With the aid of the reflector, in whose centre it is situated, it projects into space a current of peculiar nature, to which I have given the name of neuter helicoidal current. As its appellation indicates, it moves just as a revolving screw does. On the other hand, it has the property of violently repelling any material body with which it comes into contact. The aggregate of its helices constitutes a hollow cylinder, whence the air is driven out, like any other body, so that there is a vacuum inside the cylinder. Can you understand, uncle, the meaning of the word *vacuum?* Just tell yourself that while everywhere, in the infinity of space, there is *something*, my invisible cylinder, which is screwed into the atmosphere, is the only point in the universe where, for a moment or two, there is a *vacuum*. The time is very short, shorter than the duration of a flash of lightning. This unique spot where an *absolute vacuum* exists is an issue through which escapes in hurrying waves the indestructible energy held prisoner within the terrestrial globe, and condensed in the heavy meshes of matter. My rôle, therefore, limits itself to suppressing an obstacle."

Much interested, Monsieur Lecœur concentrated his attention in order to follow this curious explanation.

"The only thing which is somewhat delicate," resumed Zephyrin, after a pause, "is to regulate the neuter helicoidal current's length of wave. If it attains the object I wish to influence, it repels instead of attracting it. What is required, therefore, is that it should cease at a certain distance from the object, but as near to it as possible, in such a way that the energy liberated may radiate in the immediate neighbourhood."

"But in order to fling the bolide into the sea,

your current must repel, not attract it," objected Monsieur Lecœur.

"Yes and no," replied Zephyrin. "Pay attention, uncle. I know the exact distance separating us from the bolide. This distance is exactly five hundred metres forty-eight centimetres. I regulate the reach of my current accordingly."

Whilst speaking, Xirdal had been manipulating a rheostat intercalated in the circuit between the electric source and the machine.

"There, it's finished," he continued. "Now the current ceases less than three centimetres from the bolide, on the side of its north-east convexity. The liberated energy, therefore, surrounds it on this face with intense radiation, yet without being, perhaps, sufficient to move such a mass adhering so closely to the ground. Consequently, as a precaution, I am going to employ two subsidiary means."

Xirdal thrust his hand into the interior of the machine. Immediately one of the newly added bulbs began to crackle fiercely.

"You may remark, uncle," he said by way of commentary, "that this bulb does not revolve like the other. The reason is that the effect it produces is of a different kind. The effluvia it emits are peculiar. We will call them, with your permission, neuter rectilinear currents, to distinguish them from the preceding ones. The length of these rectilinear currents does not need to be regulated. They would go away, without being seen, into the infinite, if I did not direct them on to the south-west convex surface of the bolide, which arrests them. I don't advise you to place yourself in their path. You would catch something you wouldn't like. But to return to our subject. What are these rectilinear currents? Like the helicoidals, and, indeed, like every electric current, whatever its nature—sound, light, or heat—they are nothing else than atoms of matter carried to the utmost degree of simplification. You may gain an idea of the minuteness of these atoms when I tell you that just now they are striking the surface of the golden mass in which they fix themselves to the number of seven hundred and fifty millions per second. So it is a veritable bombardment, which compensates for the lightness of the projectiles by their infinite number and velocity. Adding this impact to the attraction exercised on the other face, we can obtain a satisfactory result."

"But the bolide is not budging," objected Monsieur Lecœur.

"It will budge," asserted Zephyrin calmly. "Have a little patience. And here is something that will hurry things up. With this third reflector I despatch other atomic howitzers, directed not against the bolide itself, but against the ground supporting it on the sea side. You will see this ground crumble gradually, and, its weight helping it, the bolide begin to slip down the incline."

Xirdal thrust his arm into the machine again. The third bulb crackled in its turn.

"Look, uncle," he said. "I think we shall have something now to assure us."

XX

Which will be read perhaps with regret, but which the author's respect for historic truth compels him to write, as one day or other the annals of astronomy will prove.

INDIVIDUAL cries blended into a general shout and developed into a roar from the crowd as the mass of gold began to shake.

Every eye was gazing in the same direction. What was happening ? Had they been the victims of an hallucination, or had the meteor really stirred ? If so, what was the cause ? Perhaps the soil was yielding a little, which might bring about the ultimate fall of the treasure into the sea.

It would be a singular ending to this affair which has so excited the world," observed Miss Arcadia Walker.

" There might be a worse one," replied Mr. Seth Stanfort.

" It would be the best," said Francis Gordon.

No, they were not mistaken. The bolide continued to slip slowly down towards the sea. Undoubtedly the ground was giving way. If this movement were not checked, the sphere of gold would roll off the plateau and be swallowed up in the ocean's depths. There was a general feeling of stupefaction, mingled with some slight contempt for this country so unworthy of the precious burden. What a pity the fall had occurred on the island instead of on the unmovable basaltic cliffs of the mainland, where these many, many milliards would not have risked being lost for ever to hungry humanity!

Yes, the meteor was slipping away. If the plateau itself should yield and crumble under the enormous weight, the whole of the bolide would be gone in a few hours, and perhaps even in a few minutes. Amidst the cries called forth by the imminence of this misfortune, those of Monsieur de Schnack were most noticeable. Adieu the opportunity that had offered itself for the milliardizing of his country! Adieu the prospect of rendering each inhabitant wealthy!

As for Mr. Dean Forsyth and Dr. Hudelson, it really seemed that they were becoming insane. They stretched out their arms wildly. They called for help, as if some one could have hindered the catastrophe. An acceleration in the bolide's movement made them lose what small reason they had left. Without thinking of the danger he was incurring, Dr. Hudelson broke through the lines of soldiers and rushed towards the sphere of gold. He was unable to go far. Stifled by the fiery atmosphere, he suddenly staggered, after running about a hundred yards, and dropped as though he had been shot.

Mr. Dean Forsyth ought to have been content, since the suppressing of his competitor suppressed all competition possible. But, before being an enthusiastic astronomer, Mr. Dean Forsyth was a good-hearted man, and, under the emotion at present experienced, his real nature regained the upper hand. His factitious hatred disappeared like a bad dream that vanishes when we awake, and in his mind and bosom there revived the reminiscence of former days. Consequently, without hesitation, just as one executes a mechanical action, Mr. Dean Forsyth—be this said to his credit—instead of waiting and rejoicing to see an adversary perish, flew bravely to the assistance of an old friend in peril. His strength was not, however, equal to his courage. He had scarcely reached Dr. Hudelson and dragged him a few yards back when he, in turn, sank down, overcome by the dreadful heat.

Fortunately Francis had rushed after him, and Mr. Seth Stanfort, too, the latter's devotion alarming Miss Arcadia Walker, for she called out instinctively: "Seth, Seth," anticipating fatal consequences to him who had been her husband.

Francis Gordon and Seth Stanfort, and some others of the braver spectators that had imitated their example, were obliged to go down on all

MR. DEAN FORSYTH . . . FLEW BRAVELY TO THE ASSISTANCE OF AN OLD FRIEND IN PERIL

fours and to cover their mouths with their handkerchiefs to protect themselves against the hot air. At last they came to the two astronomers, and, lifting them up, brought them back within the safer zone. Luckily the victims of their own imprudence had been rescued in time. Thanks to the administering of proper remedies, they were recovered from their swoon, but only to behold the ruin of their hopes.

The bolide continued to slip, either by reason of its own acquired movement or under the yielding of the soil. Its centre of gravity was nearing the edge where the cliff went sheer down into the waters beneath. On every side the crowd's excitement still manifested itself by exclamations and restlessness. Some of the spectators, with Mr. Seth Stanfort and Miss Arcadia Walker among them, ran quickly towards the sea, in order to have a better view of the plunge. At a certain moment it seemed that, after all, the golden sphere was not going to tumble. Its apparent movement ceased. But, if any one nourished hopes on this account, he was soon destined to be disappointed. An instant later there was a terrible crack. The rock had been torn off, and the meteor leapt over into the abyss.

A tremendous clamour burst from the throats of the three thousand-odd spectators, a clamour almost immediately drowned in the noise of an explosion louder than any claps of thunder.

Simultaneously an aerial tidal wave swept all the surface of the island, and every one of those watching was thrown on to the ground. The bolide had been shattered. Penetrating through the innumerable openings of the golden sponge the water had been at once turned into steam, and, rending the particles of incandescent metal asunder, had made the bolide blow up just like a boiler. Now the debris were falling in a sheaf-shaped shower upon the sea, which was itself raised by the violence of the explosion.

A tremendous swell of surf rolled on to the shore and dashed furiously over whatever resisted it. Terrified, those who had approached too near sought to run back up the slope and to put themselves in a position of safety. One at least was not successful. By the cowardly hustling of some of her companions, whose fear had transformed them into wild beasts, Miss Arcadia Walker was pushed back, caught by the swell, and thrown down. When the tide rolled back she would be inevitably carried away by it. But Mr. Seth Stanfort was there. He had seen the accident; and, risking his life, without much chance of saving the lady, he raced back to her, competing with the returning rush of water. At first it looked as though there would be two victims instead of one. However, he won the race, and, seizing the prostrate form, he scrambled with her to a rocky boulder that was near; then, clinging to it with all his strength, he managed to hold on until the mad waters had all battered them and gone by.

A number of tourists hastened at once to their assistance and bore them to the higher ground, where there was no further danger. Mr. Seth Stanfort was only a little stunned, but Miss Arcadia had fainted. Coming to herself in a short time, she thanked her preserver.

"Since I was to be saved, you were the one to do it," she said, pressing his hand, and giving him a look of the most tender gratitude.

Less fortunate than Miss Arcadia Walker, the marvellous bolide had not escaped its disastrous fate! Far from the reach of men, its debris now reposed in the briny depths, nor was there the slightest chance of their being ever found again. The nucleus having been split up by the explosion, all the myriad pieces had been scattered. Monsieur de Schnack, Mr. Dean Forsyth, and Dr. Hudelson searched in vain for some stray morsels on the shore. Not one was to be seen. They had every one been carried clear away. The milliards were nonexistent. Of the extraordinary meteor nothing remained.

XXI

A last chapter, giving the epilogue of this story, in which Mr. John Proth, the Whaston judge, says the concluding word.

THEIR curiosity being satisfied, the crowd had nothing to do now but to depart.

Was it satisfied? A doubt may be expressed as to the dénouement being worth the fatigue and expense of such a journey. To have seen the meteor only at four hundred yards' distance was a meagre result. Yet they had to be content. Could they hope to have another opportunity? Would a second golden bolide ever reappear above the terrestrial horizon? No. A thing of this kind does not happen twice. No doubt there are other golden meteors floating about in space, but the chances of their lighting upon the circle of the earth's attraction are so slight that they do not call for our serious consideration.

To tell the truth, it is no misfortune. To have a billion or two of gold suddenly added to our circulation would, out of all proportion, depreciate this metal, so vile for some—generally those who have none—and so precious for the majority.

THE TWO RIVALS HAD FORGOTTEN THEIR FORMER RIVALRY

Consequently the bolide's loss need not be regretted, since, if the matter had ended otherwise, we know not what catastrophes might have come upon the world.

Of course, those who had been most particularly interested in the bolide had some justification for feeling so disappointed. With real grief Mr. Dean Forsyth and Dr. Sydney Hudelson went to contemplate the spot where their meteor had made its bow and vanished. They were heartbroken to have to go home without a fragment of this celestial gold—not even the wherewithal to get themselves a cravat pin or a cuff stud, not even the tiniest grain that they might have kept as a souvenir, admitting that Monsieur de Schnack would not have claimed it for his country.

In their common trouble the two rivals had forgotten their former rivalry. Could they, indeed, act otherwise? Was it possible for Dr. Hudelson to be still vexed with one that had generously imperilled his own life to save him? And, on the other hand, is it not human to feel kindly towards those we have preserved from danger of death? But even without this motive, the bolide's disappearance was a sufficient reason for their becoming reconciled. What was the use of disputing about that which no longer existed?

Maybe they thought of this while they walked about arm-in-arm in the first quarter of the honeymoon of their restored friendship.

"This loss of the Forsyth bolide is a great misfortune," quoth Dr. Hudelson.

"The Hudelson bolide," corrected Mr. Dean Forsyth. "It was yours, my dear friend, yours."

"No, no," protested the doctor. "Your observation, my dear friend, preceded mine."

"On the contrary, it followed, dear friend."

"You are mistaken. The want of precision in my letter to the Cincinnati Observatory would, if need be, prove this. Instead of saying, like you, the bolide appeared from such an hour to such an hour, I said, between such an hour and such an hour. That's quite different."

The excellent doctor would not be convinced. Mr. Forsyth neither. Thus fresh discussions arose, but, happily, they were very harmless. Carried to such a point, this change of attitude had also something comic about it. Somebody, however, who did not make fun was Francis Gordon, who had now become once more Jenny's officially betrothed husband. The two young people, after so many storms, profited by the return of the fine weather and conscientiously made up for lost time.

The warships and passenger steamers anchored off Upernivik sailed during the morning of the 4th of September for more southerly latitudes. Of all the visitors who, for some days, had given so much animation to this island in the arctic regions, there remained only Monsieur Robert

Lecœur and his godson, who were forced to wait for the return of the *Atlantic*. The yacht did not arrive till the next day. The banker and Zephyrin embarked at once. They had had enough of this supplementary twenty-four hours at Upernivik. As a matter of fact, their log cabin had been destroyed by the tidal wave supervening on the bolide's explosion, and they were obliged to spend the night in the open air, under circumstances the reverse of comfortable. The sea not only razed their hut, it also wetted them through. Drying themselves as best they could in the polar sun's pale rays, they did not even possess a blanket to protect themselves from the cold during the hours of darkness. Everything had been whisked off, utensils, portmanteau, and Zephyrin's instruments to boot. Gone also the telescope with which the savant had so often gazed at the meteor. Gone also the machine that had drawn down the bolide to the earth's surface and then flung it into the ocean.

Monsieur Lecœur was inconsolable for the loss of such a marvellous apparatus. Xirdal, on the contrary, laughed. Since he had made it, nothing would prevent his making another better and more powerful one. Certainly he could have done this, had he tried. Unfortunately, he never thought any more about it. In vain his godfather urged him to start on the work. He kept putting it off and putting it off until old age came, and at length death buried his secret in the tomb.

The machine, therefore, is lost to humanity, unless another Zephyrin Xirdal should be born and reconstitute it. Zephyrin the First came back from Greenland poorer than when he set out thither. Not to speak of his instruments and his other personal belongings, he left there a large piece of land, all the more difficult to dispose of as the major portion was situated in the sea.

On the other hand, what a crop of millions his godfather had gathered in the course of the expedition! These were found duly encashed on the return to the Rue Drouot, and laid the foundations of the colossal fortune that raised Lecœur's Bank to a level of equality with the most powerful financial establishments in the world.

As Zephyrin was principally the cause of this phenomenal prosperity, Monsieur Lecœur did not fail to consult him on many other occasions. Not a few of the inventions issuing from this genius's brain were exploited by the bank, with results that were eminently satisfactory; and, failing the gold that had come down from the skies, it drained into its coffers a notable portion of that which existed on the earth.

As Monsieur Lecœur was no Shylock, it would have been easy for his godson to have his share in the cake—and that a substantial one—had he

Everything had been whisked off

so desired. But whenever the subject was touched upon, Xirdal assumed such a blank look that the banker did not insist. Money? Gold? What could he do with it? To receive at irregular intervals the petty sums that provided for his modest wants was what suited him admirably. Until the end of his life, he continued to go on foot to his godfather's bank to fetch the money that was strictly necessary, and he never consented either to quit his sixth floor in the Rue Cassette or to part with Widow Thibaut, who, until the last, was his conversation-loving Abigail.

On the seventh day after the telegram sent by Monsieur Lecœur to his Paris offices, the definite disappearance of the bolide was known all over the world. Returning from Upernivik, the French cruiser was the one to announce the news at the first signalling station; and from there the tidings spread with rapidity in all directions.

Although the event caused considerable excitement, the effects were not of long duration. The thing was finished with. The best was to forget it. In a short time people were taken up with other concerns of newer interest, and gave over thinking about the messenger from the sky, whose ending had been so deplorable, not to say ridiculous. When the *Mozik* cast anchor on the 18th of September in the port of Charleston, the affair was practically forgotten.

In addition to its outgoing passengers, the

Mozik, on her return, carried another—Miss Arcadia Walker, who, being desirous of prolonging her manifestations of gratitude to Mr. Seth Stanfort, had installed herself in the cabin left vacant by Monsieur de Schnack. From South Carolina to Virginia the distance is not great, and railways are not lacking in the United States. On the morrow, the 19th of September, Mr. Dean Forsyth, Francis, and Omicron, as also Dr. Sydney Hudelson and Jenny, entered their respective homes, the former in Elizabeth Street, the latter in Morris Street. At the Whaston station Mrs. Hudelson and Loo and the estimable Mitz were on the platform when they arrived and gave them a hearty welcome. Francis Gordon kissed his future mother-in-law, and Mr. Dean Forsyth shook hands with the same lady cordially, just as if nothing had occurred to interrupt their intimacy. No allusion, indeed, would have been made to the painful past if Miss Loo, who was still a trifle anxious, had not insisted on being reassured.

"It's finished now, anyway, isn't it?" she cried, throwing her arms round Mr. Forsyth's neck.

Yes, it was quite finished. And, as a demonstration of the fact, on the 30th of September the bells of Saint Andrew's rang their merriest peal over the Virginian city. In presence of a brilliant assembly, comprising the relatives and friends of the two families, as well as the chief people in the town, the Reverend Mr. O'Garth celebrated the marriage of Francis Gordon and Jenny Hudelson, who were at the wished-for goal, after so many trials and vicissitudes. Loo was, of course, at the ceremony in her capacity of first bridesmaid, and looked charming in her fine dress, which had been ready for the last four months. Mitz, too, was there, laughing and crying at the same time over the happiness of her sonny. Never had she been so much *removed,* she said to those with whom she spoke.

Almost at the same hour, another marriage took place elsewhere with less pomp. On this occasion, it was neither on horseback, nor on foot, nor in a balloon, that Mr. Seth Stanfort and Miss Arcadia Walker proceeded to Judge Proth's house. No, they went in a comfortable carriage, sitting side by side; and, arm-in-arm, they for the first time entered the judge's door, in order to present to Mr. Proth the requisite papers under circumstances less fantastic than on previous occasions.

The magistrate performed his duty and re-married the couple that he had divorced a few weeks before, then bowed courteously to them.

"Thanks, Mr. Proth," said Mrs. Stanfort.

"And good-bye," added Mr. Seth Stanfort.

"Good-bye, Mr. and Mrs. Stanfort," replied the judge, who forthwith returned to his garden to look after his flowers.

But a scruple troubled the worthy philosopher. As he was holding his thrice-filled watering-can in his hand, he paused and ceased to shed its beneficent shower over the thirsty geraniums.

"Good-bye! . . ." he murmured pensively, in the middle of the garden walk. "I should have done better, perhaps, to add: for the present . . ."

THE END

Printed in the United States
209957BV00001B/4/A

9 780803 296190